# "Is this where I should apologize for kissing you?" Joe asked.

There was another short silence while Sara stared out the window, not knowing what to say.

"In fact," he said at last, "if you want me to prove how unrepentant I really am, I'll pull the truck over right now and kiss you again."

The last thing she needed was another demonstration of his effect on her senses. She swung startled eyes to him as he pulled the truck onto the shoulder and calmly turned off the ignition. "What are you doing?" she demanded.

"I'm going to kiss you until you talk to me," he said matter-of-factly. He reached for her, and she stared into his handsome, open face. He ran a finger down her nose, and his voice came out a raspy whisper. "Sara, I don't want to push you into anything too fast ...But I'll be damned if I can stop myself..."

His kiss was so gentle it made her ache...

# Kelly Adams

*Though transplanted to Illinois, Kelly Adams still bears traces of her Maryland upbringing—a passion for crabcakes and the Baltimore Orioles baseball team. She has had a love affair with books from the day she first chewed on one in her crib. In sixth grade she decided to be a writer; since then she has worn out two typewriters and consumed untold quantities of chocolate in pursuit of her writing. When not writing, she diets and contemplates her hobbies—bicycling and amateur (ham) radio—but never finds time to actually indulge in them. She claims to be the world's worst housekeeper and banjo player.*

*Kelly lives with a dog with allergies and her husband, who, after more than fifteen years of marriage, often brings her a single rose to make an ordinary day special. If she ever tracks down her fairy godmother, she'll offer thanks for her incredible good fortune...*

Dear Reader:

What could be lovelier than a day in June? The next six SECOND CHANCE AT LOVE romances, of course! Jeanne Grant sets the tone by indirectly asking: Have you ever sympathized with the "other man" in romances? The guy who's nice, but ... well, he's just not the hero. Does he ever find the woman of his dreams? In *No More Mr. Nice Guy* (#340), Jeanne Grant shouts a resounding "Yes!" You see, Alan Smith is a wonderful guy, and Carroll's deeply in love with him. But sometimes she wishes he were just a little less ... well, less predictable, cautious, and controlled! And when Alan sets out to be dashing, macho, and reckless—watch out! With humor and insight, Jeanne once again creates a hero and heroine you'll simply adore ... and a one-of-a-kind love story that you'll savor and remember...

Next, Katherine Granger shows her admirable versatility in *A Place in the Sun* (#341), in which brooding, embittered Rush Mason is hired as groundskeeper by Libby Peterson, the ladylike owner of a Cape Cod inn. As Rush's powerful presence seems to shrink the lush acreage of Libby's seaside estate, their heated glances lead to sultry, sexually charged encounters that will make your own skin prickle! Slowly the tension builds ... the mystery about Rush deepens. Here's steamy reading for a warm, melting June afternoon.

What woman hasn't dreamed of meeting a dashingly handsome, thoroughly princely man who will sweep her off her feet and take her "away from all this"? In Sherryl Woods's latest romance, *A Prince Among Men* (#342), this secret desire is fulfilled for actress-mime Erin Matthews ... and the wisdom of "Be careful what you wish for because it might come true" takes on a whole new meaning! Mysterious Mark Townsend's majestic courtship of Erin will tickle your funny bone and tug on your heartstrings.

In an inspired move, Jan Mathews unites erotic dancer Cindy Marshall from her previous romance *Slightly Scandalous* (#226) and vice-squad cop Brad Jordan from *Shady Lady* (#306) to bring you another sassy, sexy romance—*Naughty and Nice* (#343). Though Cindy's now a respectable social worker, she can't forget that she once stripped for a living—and she *won't* get involved with a man as unsuitable as Brad Jordan! Easier said than done—because Brad storms all her defenses ... and in record time! No one creates tough guys like Jan Mathews ... and no one else could have written a romance as wacky and wonderful as *Naughty and Nice*.

Next, Linda Raye returns after a long hiatus with *All the Right Moves* (#344), in which two strong-willed characters find themselves on opposite sides of an issue ... and in constant disagreement over their romantic future! Basketball coach Ryan McFadden, who simply oozes sexuality, knows at once that referee Lauren Nickels is the woman for him. But Lauren's determined to remain aloof—no matter how roguish his charm or penetrating his insight! Still, Ryan sees that beneath her tough exterior there lies a woman's secret longing. With such great ingredients for romance, it's only a matter of executing all the right moves before love triumphs.

Kelly Adams has a special talent for capturing the spirit of America's heartland—both the richness of the land and the simple honesty of the people. In *Blue Skies, Golden Dreams* (#345), city slicker Sara Scott arrives on Joe Dancy's Iowa farm intending to rescue her sister from what she considers his con-artist clutches. But with lighthearted teasing, indomitable integrity, and stubborn persistence, Joe sets Sara to baking cookies and going fishing ... turning her into a country girl and stampeding her emotions in one fell swoop! In Joe's conquest of Sara, Kelly Adams conveys a breath-catching tenderness and a reaffirmation of good living that makes your heart sing.

Have a terrific June, everyone! Warm wishes,

*Ellen Edwards*

Ellen Edwards, Senior Editor
SECOND CHANCE AT LOVE
The Berkley Publishing Group
200 Madison Avenue
New York, NY 10016

# SECOND CHANCE AT LOVE™

## KELLY ADAMS
## BLUE SKIES, GOLDEN DREAMS

A
SECOND CHANCE AT LOVE
BOOK

For all the baseball players, farmers, and small-town reporters who put heart and soul into what they do

# BLUE SKIES, GOLDEN DREAMS

# Chapter One

SITTING ALONE IN the nearly deserted restaurant, Sara Scott sipped the last of her coffee thoughtfully and glanced down at the envelope resting beneath her elbow. The *Twi* of "Twin Oaks" on the return address was just visible. She had practically memorized the letter's contents.

"Don't be upset," it said. And then her sister, Carol, had gone on to do her best to upset her. Carol and her husband Eddie had been in a car accident, but they had been "taken in"—now there was a telling choice of words—by a man and his son at Twin Oaks—somewhere in the vicinity of Keokuk, Iowa. Sara had called information, assuming that Twin Oaks was an apartment building, but there was no listing for anything by that name. She had waited patiently for more word from her sister, but none came. All right, so she hadn't been pa-

1

tient. Since the letter came she had walked the length of her Chicago apartment enough times to qualify for a gold medal in rug-pacing.

This was just like Carol and Eddie! Their short married life had been marked by a long string of irresponsible fiascoes as they tried to "find themselves." Eight months ago it had been a California guru who claimed he could teach them to lower their metabolisms and put themselves into a state of suspended animation. When Sara investigated, she found out the only thing he could lower was the balance in Carol's trust fund. And then there was the con man who'd tried to sell them a shrimp farm in Arizona. Sara had rushed to Carol's side to protect her from yet another scam.

It seemed to Sara that she had been waiting forever for Carol and Eddie to, well, grow up. Shortly after Sara graduated from college, their mother died. Carol, eight years younger, had moved in with Sara. A budding career as a reporter for a Chicago newspaper had kept Sara busy, and she'd felt guilty that she didn't have the time to supervise Carol. And if anyone needed supervision, it was Carol. Neither sister had received much affection from mother or father, and Carol seemed determined to wrest her share from the whole world. Four years ago, when Carol was in college, Sara had married John Scott. Just before John was killed in a car accident a year ago, Carol graduated from college and married Eddie. Distraught by her husband's death, Sara nevertheless assured herself that Eddie was not just interested in Carol's money. She was relieved to discover that despite his dark good looks and charm he was not a fortune hunter. Quite the opposite. He wholeheartedly supported Carol's Gypsy-style day-to-day existence. He spent little money, but then he earned little, too.

Sara sighed and glanced at her reflection in the mirror behind the lunch counter. Almost unconsciously she brushed back a strand of shoulder-length, mahogany hair.

Luminous green eyes stared solemnly back at her. A slender, gamin-faced woman, at thirty-one Sara felt older than her years. Maybe it was the sense of responsibility drummed into her by her parents, the credo that she must be vigilant against all monetary interlopers. "Why didn't you give that man any money?" a five-year old Sara had asked her father one Saturday afternoon as they walked past a Salvation Army worker with a Christmas bell. Her father had just pocketed change from a hundred dollar bill after buying a box of cigars. "Never throw away money, Sara," her father admonished her. "I write them a check every year—and you'd better believe I claim it on my income taxes. I don't give it away, Sara—I work too hard to earn it."

Her parents had been equally stingy with their love. Sara's father did not dole out "loose hugs" either. Each show of affection was the profit-producing kind, given with a specific return in mind. Sara learned early that she was hugged if she got the highest grade on a test or brought home first prize in the debating contest, not if she ran home laughing, an early dandelion clutched in her hand. She frowned into the mirror, seeing traces of the solemn, well-behaved child lingering in her eyes.

Sara realized she was clutching the white envelope so tightly that she was crumpling it, and she quickly smoothed it out, studying the crude map the waitress had drawn: directions to Twin Oaks. She left the tip by her coffee cup and paid at the cash register. *Here comes Big Sister Sara galloping to the rescue again,* she mused as she made her way to her white Mustang. Ready to do battle with the father-son team of Iowa fleecers. An unlikely setting for con men, but Sara had learned a hard lesson recently: that even a seemingly trustworthy man can harbor a larcenous soul. She winced as she got in the car and a painful thought crossed her mind. Here she was racing to Carol to save her trust fund, when she herself had been taken in—by her own husband. Live and learn.

Once burned, twice cautious. She was full of trite sayings today. All learned from painful experience.

Sara frowned as she adjusted the rearview mirror. She had a plane ticket to Paris. She fully intended to use it, five weeks from now. Her apartment and her job had both seemed tedious after John's death, more so after her lawyer came to her with the unsettling news of John's "investments" of the money in her trust. She intended to wrap up Carol's problems in a few days, then return home to get ready for her trip.

She squared her shoulders and started the car. "Hi-Yo, Silver, away," she muttered disconsolately.

July in Iowa was not like July in Chicago. Despite the heat a gentle breeze ruffled the bright green stalks of corn in fields that rolled like ocean waves under a blue, never-ending sky. She had crossed the Mississippi River several miles back, and signs pointed the way to towns with names like Ottumwa and Keosauqua.

Sara frowned down at the waitress's map in her lap. She seemed to be heading farther out into the country. Strange place for an apartment complex.

The road became more rural, and she slowed down, then slammed on the brakes when she passed the entrance to a country lane nestled between two cornfields. Arching over the lane was a white sign anchored on two poles— *Twin Oaks Farm*. Sara backed up, wondering what Carol and Eddie had gotten themselves into now.

Nobody was around when she drove up the lane and stopped the car in front of a white clapboard farmhouse framed by two large oak trees. "Hello?" Sara called tentatively as she got out of the car, slinging her purse strap over her shoulder and straightening her sea-green skirt and navy print crepe blouse. A robin looked up from his perusal of the ground, and a bull bellowed in the distance. Then there was no sound other than the wind rustling the corn.

Sara took a deep breath and walked up to the front

door. She rapped firmly and waited. Nothing. She wandered past two beds of marigolds toward the back of the house, trying to remember if farmers were in the habit of letting their livestock run loose in the yard. The last thing she wanted to encounter was a territorial bull.

When she rounded the corner, Sara was surprised to see a grape arbor stretching up a hillside. She couldn't see anything beyond the cluster of thick, green leaves draped over the neatly arranged poles. She stopped and looked around, her gaze resting on a fat blue jay perched on top of a vine, his bright eye fixed on a bunch of green grapes below him. Sara smiled, reminded of a plump vintner inspecting his crop.

She froze the next instant as a decidedly masculine and triumphant voice called, "Hah! Take that, Dunbar!" *That* turned out to be a mud clod. It came sailing through the leaves just as the blue jay took to the air, screaming. The mud hit Sara on the arm, splattering the sleeve of her blouse. Her shriek of surprise mingled with the bird's mocking cries.

Sara clapped a hand over the spot where the mud had hit her, trying to soothe the sharp sting in her arm as the rustling leaves foretold someone's approach. A man stepped out from between the vines, and Sara stared.

"Aw, I'm sorry as hell," he rumbled apologetically. "I didn't know anyone was here. You okay? You look kind of stunned. You in shock or something?"

Well, yes, she was. As much from the sight of the man as from the sting of the clod of mud. He stood slightly over six feet tall. His shaggy hair was the color of corn, and a matching mustache was threaded with a tinge of gray. Blond stubble shadowed his jawline. The eyes inspecting her worriedly were an Iowa sky blue, etched with lines at the corners. He wore a bright red undershirt that he tucked hurriedly into his jeans.

"Where did I hit you?" he asked remorsefully. He had moved so close that Sara had to look almost straight up to peer into those amazing eyes. They traveled her face—looking for signs of an impending faint, she imagined—and made their way over her blouse. "Here I go and miss Dunbar completely, and end up hitting you." His eyes went to the red spot on her arm, and gentle fingers touched it, smoothing away the dirt. "Didn't break the skin," he said, "but I'll bet I gave you one dandy bruise." He glanced back at her face. "And one hell of a fright, too."

The fingers touching her arm were callused but tender; they took away the sting only to replace it with a strange churning in her bloodstream. "By the way," he said, looking into her face again, "you do talk, don't you? I haven't met a woman yet who didn't have a word or two to say on something."

Her indignation was in response not only to the teasing but also to the feelings he was arousing in her. "I have more than just a word for anyone who goes around flinging mud," she said.

He grinned in obvious delight. "Thought that might get a rise out of you. Come on. Let's get you inside and we'll clean off that arm."

Sara wasn't about to be led anywhere. She pulled her arm away to let him know. "I'm looking for someone," she said. "I really don't have time to stop and talk."

"Well, now, just who is it you're looking for? I guess it's not me?" he added hopefully.

"My sister and her husband."

"Carol and Eddie?"

"Yes," she said in surprise. What on earth was going on here?

"Well, sure. They're staying here for a while. Now, come on inside. I at least owe you a glass of iced tea. You're Sara, aren't you?" he said, his wide mouth splitting into a grin. "I'm Joe Dancy."

"Sara Scott." She was beginning to feel that Iowa was another planet. He was holding her arm again, leading her toward the back door, when something else occurred to her. "This Dunbar," she began. "Is he involved in well—a feud with you?" The last thing she needed now was to have to extricate Carol and Eddie from some kind of Hatfield-McCoy fracas.

His mouth seemed to be working to maintain a straight line. "Well, yes, you might say there's a feud between Dunbar and me. It's an old one, too. He's been stealing from me for years, now. His father started it." Her face must have registered growing apprehension, because he laughed and patted her on the back. "No cause to fret. Dunbar's a bird. A fat, sassy blue jay who tries to pick my grapes before I do."

"That bird I saw," she said in comprehension.

"That's Dunbar. He has no scruples, and I've been trying to teach him a few." He shot her another disarming grin as he opened the back door. "Hasn't impressed him in the least."

Before she had time to ponder this, she found herself inside the kitchen, and she stopped to look around. As kitchens went, this one was enormous. Even the battered pine table in the center, easily large enough to seat ten, didn't fill the space. And airy. Sunlight seemed to pour in from all six sparkling glass windows at once. There were slick scars on the wood floor where chairs had scraped back, and a blue enamel coffee pot, now faded from use, sat on the stove. She knew at once that this room was loved. It seemed to take her into its arms and enfold her.

"Tea okay?" Joe asked, his head buried in the open refrigerator.

"Yes, fine." She sat down at the table folding her hands on top. "My sister? Is she all right? She mentioned a car accident."

The head popped out of the refrigerator a moment to observe her. "You mean she didn't tell you anything other than that she was in an accident?"

"Well, she said she was all right. But nothing else."

"That's Carol." He shook his head and went back to his perusal of the refrigerator. "She worries a person to death and doesn't give it a second thought." He emerged with a pitcher of tea and a lemon. "She and Eddie are fine. They both had some cuts and scrapes, and their car still isn't fixed, but they're going to be fine." Sara noted that he gave his assurances with the proud satisfaction of a benevolent protector. "Carol says you're a reporter on a newspaper in Chicago," he said, slicing a lemon at the sink.

*"Was,"* she amended. "I quit my job. Friday was my last day. I'm leaving for Europe in a little over a month."

"Oh?" Those wayward blond eyebrows rose, and for an instant she thought she read regret in his eyes. It must have been a trick of the sunlight though; it gave his face an even more expressive, touchable look.

"I needed to get away," she explained simply.

He nodded as he set the glasses on the table and pulled out his chair. "Carol told me about your husband." He pushed the sugar bowl toward her.

Sara offered a brief prayer of gratitude that Carol didn't know John had been tampering with her money or she would have told Joe about that, too.

"Hey, I'm sorry we don't have any cookies," he said. "I think Eddie polished off the last of them this morning. They were only store-bought anyway." There was that edge of regret, again.

"This arrangement with Carol and Eddie," Sara began delicately, reminding herself of the guru. "Are they paying you rent?"

He frowned. "No, why should they?"

"Then they're working for you?"

"They seem to enjoy it. Dad and I publish a little newspaper—it used to be my mother's—and Carol and Eddie have been helping out with that. They're beginning to put down roots, I suspect. Seem to like Iowa."

The whole arrangement struck Sara as highly suspicious. In her experience, people didn't take in strangers, give them a job and house, and feed them. She was thinking guru and shrimp farm all over again. Sara was wondering if this Joe Dancy had his eye on Carol's trust fund. Undoubtedly he did.

"That's certainly generous of you," she said coolly, "allowing Carol and Eddie to move in."

"What was I supposed to do?" he asked disarmingly. "Throw dirt at them?" The sudden grin turned to an expression of concern. "Cheez, I forgot all about your arm." He was out of the chair with deceptive speed for such a big man and disappearing into another room.

Sara sat drinking her tea and frowning as she mulled over her sister's living arrangements.

"Here," he said, returning with a washcloth and a dark bottle. "Let's have a look at the damage." He gently pushed up the short sleeve of her blouse, dropping into a crouch beside her.

Sara lowered her eyes to avoid his face. Unfortunately she found herself staring at the knotted muscles in his thighs as he balanced easily on the balls of his feet. His jeans were dirt-streaked, as though he had done a lot of work in them—or dug up a lot of mud.

The touch of his hand carefully sponging off her arm with the damp cloth made her set down her glass quickly, before she spilled her tea. She felt him glance at her once before he resumed his ministrations. Her eyes moved nervously around the room, taking in the white eyelet curtains, a cheery wooden clock in the shape of a giant spoon, and a ceramic plaque on the wall over the stove: "Hassling the Cook Is Grounds for Great Bodily Harm."

She was trying to think of Carol and Eddie and how to separate them from this Iowa farmer, but she couldn't concentrate with his hand causing a riot of sensation up and down her arm. Now cut that out, she instructed her rebellious body.

He opened the bottle, and Sara coughed at the strong

odor. "I hope I don't have to drink that," she gasped.

"Not unless you want me to fetch the doctor for you," he teased. "This is liniment. It'll help take the soreness out of your muscles. Make 'em as relaxed as Jell-O."

It must have been powerful liniment. Not only did her muscles relax, but so did sinew, bone, and assorted tendons. And the effect extended well beyond her arm to her stomach and legs.

"Nothing tense about Jell-O," she murmured.

"Nope," he assented, his fingers stroking heat into her arm.

Sara found herself staring at the top of his head as he bent closer, and she smiled at the way his tousled blond hair struck out in opposite directions, like exploding fireworks. Nice thick hair. It would probably feel very soft to the touch.

Joe was chuckling, and Sara tried to recover her wits, which seemed to be scattered in five different directions around the kitchen. His hand had stilled on her arm, but he didn't remove it.

His thumb rested on a small, pink scar at her elbow, and now he stroked it gently. "Carol told me about this," he said. "Let's see now. The two of you were eating ice cream cones, but one cone fell to the sidewalk, and you and Carol got into a fight over the other one. You scraped your arm during the battle."

"Carol dropped her cone and attacked me," Sara said indignantly. "And both ice cream cones ended up on the sidewalk. Carol was only four at the time, and I was twelve, so I got the blame."

Joe was grinning, leaning back to look up at her face. "I heard about the ice skating accident, too. You were showing off in front of a high school boy, and you fell down and cut your leg just above the knee." His eyes moved speculatively to the vicinity of her knee—well, actually quite a bit above the knee—and Sara self-consciously tugged her skirt down.

"What's Carol been doing, showing home movies?"

He shook his head and stood up, still grinning. "No, she just likes to talk about you. Can't say I blame her."

"So," she said, trying to keep things light, "let's not spread the word about my scars, okay?"

"That's a promise," he said solemnly, crossing his heart with the liniment bottle. He set the bottle on the counter and shoved his hands into his jeans pockets, leaning back against the sink. "Listen, you're going to like it here. We don't have all those cultural things here like you have in Chicago, but this isn't a wasteland. There are plenty of art programs and theaters and museums in the state, even though we're pretty rural right here."

He shifted position, and it suddenly dawned on Sara that he looked very tired. It also occurred to her, much to her discomfort, that he expected her to stay at the farm.

"And," he was continuing, "we've got some dandy fishing up north. Hell, some of our trout can walk off with your car. And I want you to see our little newspaper. We're real proud of that."

"Joe—" She tried to interrupt him. She didn't know him or his family or even how many people lived in this house.

"'Course the paper's nothing like what you're used to," he said with no decrease in enthusiasm. "It's only a weekly, and it's pretty folksy. Dad doubles as editor-in-chief and ad salesman, and I help out when I'm not too busy with the farm."

"I don't know—"

"There's plenty of room here, Sara. Dad and I aren't the most formal people you'll meet. You can come and go as you please. Life moves at a slower pace out here, so you can just relax." He glanced out the window at the sound of a car. "And here comes your sister now. So let's not argue in front of her."

"I'm not arguing," she began in exasperation, but her words were lost as the screen door slammed.

Suddenly Carol was tugging Sara to her feet and hugging her and laughing at the same time. "Why didn't you let me know you were coming?" she squealed in delight. Curly brown hair tumbled about her face. She was a girlish, less polished version of Sara. "I was wondering whose car was in the drive, and then we got closer, and I said, 'Look, Eddie, that's Sara's car!' Didn't I?" She glanced at Eddie, who had followed her in and now stood by the door in his short-sleeved sweat shirt and jeans, grinning.

"You sure did," Eddie said, nodding nonstop. Sara held out her hand, and Eddie came forward and squeezed it affectionately. "Good to see you, Sis."

Eddie's heart was in the right place, even if he was pretty much an irresponsible drifter, and Sara forgave him the "Sis." "How could I let you know I was coming?" she chided Carol when her sister stopped for breath. "You didn't give me a phone number or any return address other than Twin Oaks, somewhere near Keokuk, Iowa."

"Oh, yeah." Carol laughed and shrugged. "Well, I didn't want you to worry. Especially after California."

"Telling me you were in a car accident and not to worry does not have a calming effect," Sara informed her. She darted a glance at Joe, wondering if he'd caught the mention of California, but he was still leaning against the sink, smiling benevolently down on this family reunion. He met her eyes briefly, and Sara looked away first.

"Eddie was driving late at night, and he fell asleep at the wheel. We ran off the road and hit a fence." Carol grimaced. "But everything worked out. It was Joe's fence. His dad got us to the hospital, and Joe towed our car back here."

"Hospital?" Sara cried in alarm.

Carol hugged her again. "Just to be checked over. We

had a few bruises. The car wasn't as lucky as we were. But Joe's been working on it. Eddie says—"

"There's no need for Joe to work on your car," Sara interrupted quickly. "You could have it done at a garage."

"Joe likes to work on cars," Eddie said enthusiastically. "He insisted we stay here, too. He wouldn't take a cent."

"Imagine that," Sara said faintly, meeting Joe's eyes again over Carol's shoulder. Joe was apparently subtler than the guru. In exchange for a healthy bite of Carol's trust, the pundit had promised to relieve them of their earthly worries. It had taken Sara two days with an army of lawyers to get things straightened out.

"Have you seen the farm?" Carol demanded, releasing Sara and opening the refrigerator. "And the newspaper? No, I guess you couldn't have. Eddie and I just came from there. We've been helping J.D. with pasteups."

"J.D.?"

"My dad," Joe said from the sink. "And I'm afraid I didn't give Sara the most gracious welcome. I tossed a clod of mud at Dunbar, and I got Sara instead."

Carol plopped down on a kitchen chair with a glass of tea, grinning. "So you've met Dunbar."

"We weren't actually introduced." Sara smiled.

"Joe's been trying to get that bird forever. You should hear his dad tell the story. They call him Dunbar because that's the name of some guy who always tried to steal second base on Joe." At Sara's blank look, Carol added, "Joe was a catcher with the Orioles."

Sara drew another blank, but she felt the need to say something with all three pairs of eyes on her. "Orioles?" she repeated dumbly.

Joe was grinning as he pulled up a chair and sat down, stretching out his long legs. He still looked tired, and Sara couldn't take her eyes off his face as he raked a hand through that thick hair. "Baseball, Sara. The Baltimore Orioles are a team in the American League Eastern

Division. I played with them for five years, not counting
Triple A."

"J.D. says he could have played another five years if
his knees had held up."

These terms were swimming in Sara's head. American
League? Triple A? Wasn't that an auto club?

"He was dating that pantyhose heiress," Carol said in
the confidential tone of a woman addressing her hair-
dresser. "You know, the one whose family designed hose
made of hemp? They didn't get married, though."

"Apparently I'm not as attractive out of uniform. And
with manure on my boots," Joe added dryly, and Sara
caught the edge in his voice. He stood up and dusted off
his jeans. "Well, Sara doesn't want to hear boring baseball stories. I'll get her suitcase and show her to her
room."

Sara opened her mouth to protest, but Joe apparently
anticipated it. He held up a hand to stop her. "Number
one, it's no trouble," he said, ticking off on his fingers
the reasons why she should stay. "Number two, the motel
is half an hour's drive. Number three, I don't trust that
motel to take good care of you, and number four—" He
rubbed his stubbly chin and pondered the final reason.
"And number four," he repeated, eyes twinkling, "I bet
you've never stayed in an Iowa farmhouse." Satisfied,
he left to get her bag.

No, she had never stayed in any farmhouse, much
less one in Iowa that was owned by a handsome former
baseball catcher.

And number five, she was going to have to get him
alone and have it out with him—bluntly—on financial
matters. Just what did he want from her family?

# Chapter Two

JOE HAD TAKEN her to a room on the second floor. It boasted a twin bed, a hardwood floor with a large braided rug, and youthful wallpaper patterned with baseball players arrayed in various positions, batting, throwing, and catching.

She had just changed from her mud-splattered suit into a clean skirt and blouse in shades of red when Joe thumped on the door, demanding to know if she could stir soup.

"Of course I can stir soup," she said, and he promptly opened the door.

"Is that all you have to wear?" he said, eyeing her.

Sara bristled. "So glad you like it. Fortunately, some men do. I got four winks and a leer the last time I wore this."

Joe was grinning. "You Chicago women sure are a feisty lot. I just don't think you're going to be very comfortable that dressed up. And if you want a wink or a leer, I'd be glad to oblige."

"No, thank you. I think I can survive without that."

He stood scrutinizing her a moment longer, shaking his head sadly when his eyes dropped to her high heels. "No, no. Those won't do at all."

"And why not? Don't they conform to the dress code?"

"Not around here. Look, don't go getting upset. But to stir the soup you've got to stand on your feet, and you'll keel over on the floor in those. Wait here."

He disappeared, and Sara stood in the middle of the room glaring indecisively at the open door. Now what?

"These aren't fashionable, but they're comfortable. You won't have to soak your feet tonight if you wear them." His voice rumbled from his chest like fudge coming to a boil as he strode unceremoniously into the room. Dangling from his hand was a pair of battered white sneakers. "Seven and a half, right?" he said confidently.

"Six," she informed his archly. "And if you think I'm going to wear those—"

"Now, there you go getting upset. All I'm trying to do is save you from aching feet," he said reasonably, stepping closer until Sara sat down on the edge of the bed. "I know these look a little shopworn, but I swear they've never been within kicking distance of a compost pile." He held up one sneaker as if about to deliver it to her nose for proof, and Sara shook her head quickly. Apparently taking that as acquiescence, Joe knelt before her and slipped off her shoes. "My mother used to wear these when she was working late at the paper. Said they were more comfortable than slippers." He was putting the sneakers on her feet, tying the laces as he spoke, but Sara's thoughts became a jumble of confusion at the touch of his fingers on her ankle. A protest died in her throat, caught on the aching lump there. She was startled that big, callused hands like this farmer's could make her feel so strangely warm and lonely at the same time. She'd never experienced such a surge of heat under John's smooth-skinned touch. She immediately suffered a pang of guilt—though why, she wasn't sure.

The room swam back into focus, and she realized she was staring down at Joe's upturned face. What was more, he was returning her stare as though patiently following her thoughts. His features were as rough as his hands and equally compelling. His nose was slightly crooked— probably broken once—but he had the kind of sharp beautiful bone structure that made her want to caress his cheek with her palm. Those grave blue eyes never left her face, as if Sara's thoughts were the most important thing in the world to this man. That ruddy glow over his tan made them bluer still. John's eyes were brown, and the last two years they were married his gaze seldom met hers directly. *Afraid of what we might find in each other's faces,* she thought wearily.

"There you go, Cinderella," Joe said softly, his fingers leaving her ankle with seeming reluctance. "All set for the ball."

He stood up and jammed his hands in his pockets, and Sara caught a fleeting glimpse of sadness on his face. She pretended not to notice. "And my coach?" she said lightly.

"Plenty of pumpkins in the field," he answered, a hint of a smile playing around his lips.

"A horse to pull the coach?"

He nodded. "Couple of broken down mares grazing in the back twenty."

"And Prince Charming's here, too, I suppose?" She was sorry she'd said it when that fleeting expression crossed his face again. He looked as if he'd had a lot of highs and lows in his life, and he'd weathered both with equanimity. What he was going through now she didn't know.

He spoke carefully. "It's always possible, I guess. Anything is."

Neither spoke for a moment, and Sara could hear the breeze rustling the corn again. Somewhere behind the house a cow bellowed mournfully.

"I've got to get cleaned up," Joe said abruptly. "I'll see you in the kitchen. Dad ought to be bringing the company any time now."

"Company?" she repeated, not sure she was ready to cope with this. She was dead tired, and the last thing she needed was to have to smile and think of polite things to say for an evening filled with more strangers.

"You might say they're railroad men," he said, grin firmly back in place.

She just stared at him. What was he talking about? Engineers? Conductors? What?

"You come back here and explain yourself," she called after him with more than a trace of impatience as he backed out of the room, laughing. Of course he didn't listen.

She sighed in exasperation. She might as well go stir the soup or whatever it was he wanted her to do. She stared down at the sneakers in distraction. One nylon-covered toe protruded through a hole in the end. Another hole at the side was fraying away from the rubber rim, and her little toe was visible through that. And naturally he'd been right about the size. They were almost a perfect fit.

In the kitchen she found a recipe for corn chowder on the counter and the ingredients more or less stacked next to it. "Stir the soup, he said," she muttered to herself. "He said nothing about making it from scratch." Was this what women did in Iowa? she wondered. Made soup from scratch and talked to themselves? Probably, if they knew Joe Dancy.

She was cutting fresh corn from the cob when he came

back to the kitchen forty-five minutes later, his hair damp and smelling clean as he drew close. He was dressed in a new pair of jeans that hugged his lean hips and a freshly pressed blue denim shirt with the sleeves rolled up to the elbows. "Smells good," he said, lifting the lid on the pot to sniff the potatoes and onions she had browned in salt pork.

She glanced up to deliver a tart retort about the difference between stirring the soup and making it single-handedly when she stopped in her tracks, eyeing him wordlessly. Why he'd shaved—and trimmed his mustache! She swallowed hard as her eyes swept his face. Lord, he was handsome! Corn wasn't all they knew how to grow in Iowa. They were pretty good at men, too.

His smile was tentative when he encountered the expression on her face, and he slowly lowered the lid to the pot. "Sara," he said, half quizzically, stepping so close she could smell the faint scent of after shave, something woodsy. His fingers grazed hers on the counter, hesitantly at first, and then gently closing over her hand. His hand was so large that she felt lost in it. Lost but safe.

"Sara," he began again, "I'm glad you're staying."

She was unable to speak for a minute. "Just for a little while," she said finally, the pounding of her heart underscoring the words.

He tightened his mouth but nodded. What worried her was that determined glint in his eyes. Apparently he had more in mind than just a night. Bitterly, Sara wondered how many nights her own trust fund—or what remained of it—would buy.

The thought seemed mercenary and cold in this big, warm kitchen, but she was not one to shy away from life's cold realities. Not since John's death, when she'd been forced to cope with the vagaries of everyday living alone. Not after a lawyer wrote to say her husband had done some "questionable things" with her money. Sara had learned in a hurry to grit her teeth and keep moving, one step at a time.

At the sound of a door slamming in the drive, Joe moved away and busied himself slicing potatoes into a skillet of melted butter. The screen door slammed, and Sara turned from the counter. A tall, lean man with thick graying hair and a ready smile came in first. He was wearing dress denims and a white shirt, and Sara saw the family resemblance at one.

"Dad," Joe said, grinning over his shoulder as he continued to slice potatoes, "I want you to meet Carol's sister, Sara Scott."

"Why, I'm pleased to meet you," Joe's father drawled, immediately striding over to Sara and shaking her hand, which was still damp from the corn. "It's a good thing you came out. Otherwise Joe might have been on his way to Chicago."

Sara glanced from his twinkling blue eyes to Joe's crooked smile before Joe turned his attention back to the potatoes.

"Carol had a tin of your cookies when she first got here, and she gave a few to Joe. Never saw him take to anything quite like that in my life. He was mighty interested in that photo of you that Carol showed him, too."

"I'm glad he liked the cookies, Mr. Dancy," Sara said, her eyes straying back to Joe. He wouldn't look at her.

"Call me J.D., honey. Don't answer to anything else. Now, you come here and meet the boys." J.D. hollered toward the door. "Get in here, fellas, and stop rubbing the welcome mat raw."

The screen door opened again, and three men trooped in, grinning and shuffling their feet on the wood floor. Sara stared—she just couldn't help it. They looked like vagrants; there was just no other way to put it. Of varying ages, they were similar only in threadbare appearance.

"Now, this here is Ron the Runner." He drew forward a wraithlike young man with shaggy coal black hair and a loose-limbed gait. His faded, torn jeans hung slackly from a cracked leather belt. His T-shirt said "I'm a Ramblin' Man." Sara had no trouble believing that.

"Nice to meet you, ma'am," Ron the Runner said softly. "I like your shoes."

Sara flushed as she glanced down at her sneakers. She shook the frail hand he offered.

She was still in a state of bewilderment as J.D. introduced the other two, an old man with a cane, wearing worn striped trousers with a plaid jacket, and another young man who was bald but sported a blond beard big enough to roost two hens. The old man was Jumping Jones, and the blond beard was Skinny Sam. Jumping Jones didn't look as if he did much jumping anymore, and Skinny Sam weighed two-fifty if he weighed an ounce, but Sara took the introductions in stride.

Jones thumped his cane on the floor and directed a few words at Joe, who was drying his hands at the sink and grinning over the proceedings. "Damned if you don't look smart, boy. Now, what's the occasion?"

Joe looked embarrassed. "Seeing you three again's all the occasion I need, Jonesie."

"Naw." Jones waved aside Joe's explanation with his cane. "Them's new pants, ain't they?"

"Say, you're right," J.D. said, running the back of his hand over his mouth to hide his smile. "That shirt's just off the rack, too. And you shaved, didn't you, Joe?"

"Man, must be someone special, right?" Ron the Runner rocked on his heels as he poked his tongue against his cheek thoughtfully.

"None of your business," Joe said good-naturedly. "Now, you all want to take some lemonade out on the porch or what?"

All four left the kitchen after a great deal of lip smacking over Joe's appearance.

Sara eyed Joe warily as she stirred milk and cream into the chowder. "All right, Dancy," she said at last when he steadfastly refused to meet her gaze. "Ron the Runner and Jumping Jones? Who are these men—fugitives from the law? Skinny Sam is a counterfeiter, right?"

Joe was laughing and blithely turning potatoes. "Nope. They're hoboes."

"Hoboes?" She stared at him in surprise.

Joe was obviously relishing her reaction as he leaned against the counter to survey her, chin tucked in. "Ron and Jones ride the rails. Sam's employed full-time as a stockbroker. He takes a long vacation every summer to join them."

"I'm not sure I'd buy a stock on that man's recommendation," Sara murmured weakly.

"He's one of the best," Joe assured her. "Next month is the National Hobo Convention in Britt. That's up in the northern part of the state. The townspeople elect a king and queen of the hoboes every year. These guys are working their way up there." He began dropping fat sausages into another skillet and pointed toward a cupboard. "Think you can set the table? We're just about ready to eat."

She managed to find everything, and fifteen minutes later they were all gathered around the table enjoying a dinner of sausage, fried potatoes, applesauce, bread, and corn chowder. Carol had baked a cherry pie the night before, and when the table was cleared Eddie and Joe took turns cranking an ice cream maker while they all sat on the front porch.

"Ya know, Joe," Jumping Jones said laconically, leaning back in his chair and chomping down on the unlit cigar he kept perpetually in his mouth, "the Runner and me just ran into that gal that took such a liking to you at the state fair few years back."

Joe grunted noncommittally as he turned the crank.

"We was hopping a freight train out of Cedar Rapids—couldn'ta been more'n a month ago—and we stopped at a café there to get some coffee. She was the waitress."

"Pretty little thing," Ron the Runner chimed in with his soft voice. "Asked about you when she saw us."

"Yeah," Jones said slowly, taking his cigar out of his mouth to study it, a fleck of tobacco clinging to his lower lip. "She said she was turning the countryside over looking for you."

Joe stood up slowly and turned the ice cream over to Eddie. With a hard stare directed toward Jones, he said, "I'll get the bowls."

Jones and the Runner exploded in laughter, slapping their thighs, as the door banged behind Joe. "That little thing sure took a liking to Joe," Jones said, smiling. "Never saw a man could twist a lady around his little finger like your boy, J.D."

"More women than you can shake a stick at," the Runner echoed. "They all go ape over baseball players."

"That's the problem," J.D. said, resting his feet on the porch rail, his arms crossed behind his head. "Seems like the women all want a sports hero and not a farm boy, and that doesn't sit well with Joe."

"If I had the ladies hanging on my shirttails like that," Jones said wistfully, "I think I'd buy me a little cottage and retire from hoboing. Just let 'em line up outside my door and take a number."

"Take a number to knock you on your empty head," Joe groused as he pushed open the door with his foot. He set the bowls by the ice cream canister, and Eddie pulled out the paddles, dripping with thick, white cream.

"What happened with those two girls who drove out last summer to get their baseballs signed?" Sam asked.

Joe looked weary. "They giggled and wanted to know what it was like to play on a team that won a World Series, and then one of them asked if I was going to do underwear ads like the other players."

Jones hooted. "Hell, no, not with your busted knees, boy."

Ron grinned widely, displaying a gold tooth. "I don't rightly know as if I agree with that, Jonesie. If they shaved his legs, damned if Joe couldn't do one of those pantyhose ads like Joe Namath did."

"Now maybe that's what that pantyhose heiress had in mind, Joe," Jonesie said, rubbing his grizzled chin and cackling.

Joe smiled with good-natured tolerance, stopping by Sara to hold out a bowl as the group howled over their jests. His hands were so big that her fingers grazed his as she took it. She felt the warm flush steal up her face.

The talk turned to other things, and Sara listened drowsily. The night air was cool, and she curled one sneakered foot under her and hugged her arms to her chest. Joe went inside for a minute and returned with a sweater, which he wrapped around her shoulders wordlessly. She looked at him solemnly, her mind filled with stories of the apparently endless procession of women in his life. She reminded herself that she had no intention of joining the parade of adoring females; she was here strictly to protect Carol and Eddie.

She nearly fell asleep listening to the cadence of the hoboes telling their stories of life on the trains. But the image recurring in her head was of a tall, blond man with gentle blue eyes who had looked so sad as he put his sweater around her.

Night had settled over the farm when they all went inside. Crickets chirped away in the yard, and a whippoorwill warbled by the road where an occasional pickup truck rumbled past.

J.D. showed the three hoboes to their rooms on the first floor, and Sara climbed the stairs to her own room after calling a sleepy good night to everyone. Carol and Eddie had already disappeared up the stairs, arms around each other.

"Sara?"

She turned. Joe stood at the foot of the stairs, hands in his back pockets. He seemed to be searching for something to say. "Do you like anything special for breakfast?" he asked finally, looking at the stairs but not at Sara.

She shook her head. "No, thanks."

He cleared his throat. "Sara, that talk tonight about . . . Well, it was just a bunch of tomfoolery. An eligible bachelor in these parts generates as much speculation as a grand champion hog. And a lot less respect."

She managed a smile. "Joe, I am definitely not interested in your love life, past or present."

He drew a deep breath, a frown creasing his forehead. "Okay." He hesitated again. "Well, get a good night's sleep." He was still standing at the foot of the stairs when she reached the top and looked back.

Sara sank down on the single bed, and sat without moving for several minutes. She was going to have to confront Joe about Carol and Eddie—and herself. She didn't want to do it, but there was something that had to be said. If it was money Joe wanted . . .

There was something else she didn't want to think about, but it had become a nightly ritual with her. She pulled the worn letter from her purse and lay back, slowly reading it in the light from the little lamp by the bed: "Dear Mrs. Scott, I regret to inform you that there are irregularities concerning your husband's estate. Please call for an appointment to discuss this matter at your earliest convenience."

And attached to the impersonal letter were several photocopied documents, hard evidence that John, during the four years of their marriage, had slowly been draining Sara's trust, investing in shaky projects that fell through, taking out informal loans, running up gambling debts. Sara had authorized the lawyer to settle the money John owed, then had asked him point-blank about John's dealings. The lawyer had confirmed—all the time looking at the papers on his desk and not at Sara—that had John continued in this mismanagement of her trust, it would have been gone in less than ten years.

Sara Scott, who had learned hard financial lessons from her parents, had almost lost her entire inheritance to the one man she had loved and trusted.

# Chapter Three

As a graduate of the Lone Ranger School of Would-Be Rescuers, Sara liked to operate efficiently and anonymously, riding into town quietly, extricating Carol and Eddie from their latest financial crisis, then departing into the sunset while bemused townsfolk murmured in awe, "Who was that masked woman?" She considered her dispatch of the guru one of her better efforts. She had arrived at the "religious retreat" on a Thursday, quickly sized up the situation, and asked her lawyers to call the guru and explain to him the definition of "fraud." On Friday Sara was on her way back to Chicago, satisfied with a job well done.

For some indefinable reason, her plan for dealing with Joe Dancy had bogged down last night. By now she should be crisply explaining that if he had any intention of getting his callused hands on Carol's trust, he might as well pack it in. She, Sara Scott, had foiled bigger operators than an Iowa farmer. But Joe Dancy had something that none of the other con artists had had—an appealing veneer of innocence. She swiftly buttoned her yellow silk blouse, brushed one hand over the matching skirt, and told herself that John had had the same kind of appeal. And look where that had gotten her! Apparently John began his financial maneuverings the minute she married him. He had worked in a small textbook publishing house, and his assets were far more modest than Sara's. She knew what that could do to a male ego, so she had made him co-trustee of her inheritance and agreed that he manage the money. She could have forgiven him the bad investments, even the "emergency" loans. The gambling was harder. He had cheated her not just of money but also of her faith in people. Even after four months, she hadn't recovered from the shock of her lawyer's discovery.

She faced herself in the mirror like a drill sergeant issuing orders to the troops. "You, Sara Scott," she muttered, "will stop this silly procrastination and set Joe Dancy straight today." Surely he expected something in return for taking in Carol and Eddie. Maybe she could work out a small cash settlement with him.

Thus fortified, she headed downstairs to the kitchen. Joe surveyed her from her sleeked-back hair to her low-heeled sandals, one eyebrow cocked. Ignoring his look, Sara pointedly laid the folded sweater and old sneakers on the hutch.

She had just poured herself a cup of coffee and taken a doughnut from the box on the counter when Joe whacked her backside with a baseball cap and called cheerfully, "Come on, kid. Let's get going."

"What?" she demanded around a mouthful of doughnut. "Where?" she managed through a last sip of coffee as Joe took her arm and propelled her to the door.

"They're waiting for us," Joe informed her.

"Who?" She managed to stuff the last of the doughnut in her mouth.

He stopped dragging her in his wake and turned to grin at her. "You ask a lot of questions, don't you? Come on. We're taking the guys to the railroad yard."

He was pulling her by the arm again, but she went on trying to extract information from him. "Where are Carol and Eddie? And your father?"

"They've left for the newspaper office already. Did you want to take notes or shall we get going?"

She'd hoped for a station wagon or, lacking that, a car with plenty of leg room. What she got was a bright red pickup with a loose tailgate that rattled and clanged with every one of the forty-two bumps on the road to the rail yard. Sara counted them, because each one was a momentous occasion, throwing her first to the left against Joe, who was driving, and then to the right, against Jumping Jones. By the thirtieth bump, she had grown accustomed to the scratchy touch of Jones's jacket as she hit his shoulder and the rancid odor of the cigar that must have steeped in his mouth for the last four months. What she couldn't get used to, even by the forty-second bump, when they finally pulled into the rail yard, was the feel of hard muscle each time her leg grazed Joe's. It caused a heated longing in her stomach and a wayward thought of how those rough, sinewy hands on the steering wheel might feel on her bare skin.

When Jones got out, his only words were "Damn, if I were twenty years younger. Oh, hell, I'd settle for ten." He rapped on the back of the truck with his cane, and the Runner and Skinny Sam clambered out, giving a last wave to Joe and Sara as they trotted toward a freight train rolling slowly past.

Sara's last impression of the rail yard just before Joe pulled away was the sound of that metal monster rolling over the tracks and the mournful clang of a bell. All around the yard, cars and engines sat idly on tracks like so many toys of a giant. Sara glanced back and saw the three hoboes hoisting themselves into an empty freight car on the moving train.

She and Joe rode in silence while Sara tried to gather her courage to broach the subject of finances. She had moved to the right after Jones got out, but not all the way—the odor of his cigar still lingered in the air like a smelly apparition.

Sara cleared her throat. "I need to talk to you."

Joe made an unintelligible sound in his throat. "Figured you did." He was staring ahead, brows creased in a straight line. The hair showing under his cap was tousled from the wind blowing in the open window, and his eyes were a deep blue against his tanned face. She experienced an empty ache just looking at him.

"Joe," she began again, "about Carol, Eddie, and me."

He held up one hand. "Wait a minute. We're not having any long, serious discussions until we settle a couple of things."

"What?"

"This, for one." He pulled the truck into a small shopping center, consisting of five stores, and slapped the steering wheel with his palm. "Come on. We have some shopping to do."

Protest was futile, also lost in the clean scent of his hair as he reached across her to open her door, his arm brushing her thigh. Sara was riveted to the seat by that same, sudden longing. Joe was already out of the truck and humming off-key by the time she finally moved.

"What goes into those cookies of yours?" he demanded cheerfully, taking her hand in his and pulling her into the cool confines of a small grocery store.

"Flour, sugar, anise oil," she said in a daze. "Eggs."

Joe piloted a cart in front of them, intent on his mission. Ten-pound sacks of flour and sugar were mere feathers in his big hands. "Anise oil," he said, thoughtfully perusing the shelf of spices. "Ah." He lowered those items into the cart and grinned.

Sara crossed her arms and regarded him with pursed lips. "Think you can handle all this baking?" she asked.

"I was hoping you might help," he said with a self-effacing smile that Sara knew was calculated to melt her heart. And it was working.

She glanced over the pile of groceries in the cart. "You have enough stuff here to keep someone baking from now until Christmas."

"That's the idea," he said cheerfully.

"Joe," she said seriously. "Listen."

"Not now," he said, placing one lean, strong finger against her lips to enforce his order. "What else do you need?"

Sara sighed in exasperation. "Hartshorn."

"What's that—an aphrodisiac?" He gave her a broad leer and twirled his mustache between finger and thumb. "Maybe I ought to double the recipe."

"It's the leavening," she explained, ignoring his attempt at humor. "It's ammonium carbonate. A drugstore would have it."

"Then it's on to the drugstore," he said, pushing the cart toward the checkout.

"Hey, Joe," said the rotund, bright-eyed woman at the cash register. She was about fifty, and the expression on her face indicated that her feet were in a perpetual state of soreness. "Did you come down the highway? Heard a hog truck overturned."

"No, we took the back way. Anybody hurt?"

The woman shook her head. "It took the sheriff's department two hours to round up all the pigs, though. Even Earlene went out there after her shift to help."

"She must have been a sight. Chasing pigs!"

The woman laughed, her mouth large and generous. "Caught one, they said." She darted Joe a sly look. "Guess that porker wasn't as slippery as you."

Joe smiled. "You know how a man feels about being chased, Della. He wants to stay far enough ahead of the woman to keep from getting caught, but close enough to let her tug on his shirt now and then."

Della finished bagging the groceries and winked at Joe. "One of these days your running shoes are gonna give out, Joe, and you *are* gonna get caught."

"Hope so, Della," he said, heading for the door. "Sure hope so." Della's laughter followed them out the door.

"What are you, the local legend?" Sara said stiffly, blinking in the sudden sunshine. "Was Earlene your latest pursuer?"

Joe grinned as he stowed the bag of groceries on the front seat of the truck. "Earlene is the radio dispatcher for the sheriff's department," he said over his shoulder. "We were both in the potato sack race at the children's home benefit last year. She kept pulling on my shirt, though." He straightened up and shut the truck door with a flourish. "She's sixty-four years old." He snapped his fingers and gave a mock grimace of regret. "But I forgot. You're not interested in the women in my life."

"That's right, I'm not," she returned. "Of all the arrogant—"

"Now let's not have a quarrel in front of the whole town, honey," Joe said mildly, and she knew he was thoroughly enjoying himself. He pushed a five dollar bill into her hand and turned her away from him, hands on her shoulders. "Drugstore's that way. I've got to pick up something in the general store."

If he patted her on the head, she would do him physical damage! But he didn't, and she had no excuse to deck him in full view of four old men sitting on a bench in front of the general store, whittling and looking as if they'd been nailed into place with the building. Instead, Joe let his hand trail lightly down her back. Sara swung around, but he had already darted out of harm's way. He smiled over his shoulder as he hopped up to the sidewalk. Sara headed for the drugstore. If he thought she gave one whit about any of his female conquests, then he was wrong, buster.

She was sitting primly in the truck when he emerged from the general store, a large bag under one arm. That crooked grin of his started the minute he saw her, but Sara deliberately kept her eyes on the four whittlers.

He slid onto the seat and tossed his cap onto the dashboard. "I'm sorry I got you mad, Sara," he said, grinning at nothing in particular. He was apparently trying to sound contrite, though he didn't much look it. "But you're the cutest little thing. Your hair all pinned up like that and your pretty skirts and blouses. Hell, you look like a Sunday school teacher I had once. I couldn't help riling her either."

Oh, he was riling her all right. But Sara was determined to ignore him. With one more sideways grin he started the engine and pulled out onto the road.

He persisted in humming tunelessly until they stopped at a gas station. The gas cap was on her side, and he leaned one arm on the roof of the truck, resting his forehead on it, his face close to the open window, while the pump merrily ticked off dollars and cents. She wouldn't look at his face so close to her own. No way. Not even if he started that damn humming again.

"Want a soda?" he asked conversationally.

Sara shook her head. "No, thank you."

He brushed aside a strand of her hair. "Do you always control yourself so carefully?" he asked, and at the unexpected question she swung around to face him.

"What?"

"What's the matter, Sara? What are you trying not to feel?"

She couldn't answer him, not while she was staring into those eyes that seemed to contain the whole world. How could he accuse her of not feeling when the finger stroking her hair was like a lightning bolt to her nerves? She was acutely aware of every sensation; even the soft breeze carrying a scent of honeysuckle was indelibly etched in her memory. She would never forget that scent, or how blue Joe's eyes were. How gently they watched her, how incredibly alive she felt as his finger traced the line of her cheek. Without thinking, she raised her face to his.

His kiss was so gentle that it made her ache. The rough hands were tender as they framed her face and turned it up to his. His mouth covered hers, softly, almost hesitantly, as if this sudden flame between them was special to him. Sara lost herself in the kiss, in the way his lips moved over hers, his tongue gentling open her mouth to seek her warmth and spark her desire, in the restless movement of his fingers on her cheek, stroking her with infinite care. She answered him with a quick, fierce rush of desire, her hands tangling in his hair. Her tongue made love to his, igniting deeper fires. He murmured softly against her lips, but it was more a sound of pleasure than a word. His hair reminded her of silky-tassled corn, fresh and wild. And, like an Iowa breeze, his fingers roved her face and neck, eliciting a small sound from deep within her throat.

The gas pump shut itself off with a loud click that suddenly reminded Sara she was sitting in a pickup truck at a little filling station on Main Street. A nosy population was driving past, and no doubt gaping at her public display.

Apparently sensing her embarrassment, Joe backed away. "It's okay," he said, smiling. "Anybody looking this way was probably just trying to read the free gift of the month."

Over his shoulder she saw a sign suspended between two pumps: "Free Glass with every Fill-up—Two Glasses with Oil Change and Lube."

Shaking her head, she smiled. And then mentally shook

herself. She had the feeling she was on another planet and had left her mind behind on blast-off. This man might have designs on Carol's money! And here she had let him kiss her in full view of half of Iowa. And what did Joe Dancy want from her?

He got in the cab and handed her a glass. Sara turned it over and read, "Frank's Fertilizer, The One with Pow."

"Should say 'power' instead of 'pow,'" Joe said casually. "The printing company charged by the letter, and Frank figured 'pow' was good enough." He glanced at her sideways, his mouth curved in amusement, and Sara managed a smile.

They rode in silence, Joe staring ahead thoughtfully.

"Is this where I should apologize for kissing you?" he asked at last, his voice not abrupt but definitely wary. "I'm not going to, you know."

There was another short silence while Sara stared out the window uncomfortably, not knowing what to say.

"In fact," he said at last, "if you want me to prove how unrepentant I really am, I'll pull the truck over right now and kiss you again."

The last thing she needed was another demonstration of his effect on her senses! She told herself she had enjoyed Joe Dancy's kiss because she was lonely; she hadn't been thinking straight. She didn't want her attraction to him to mean any more than that! She didn't want to join the list of females who clung to Joe's shirttail . . .

She swung startled eyes to him as he pulled the truck onto the shoulder and calmly turned off the ignition. "What are you doing?" she demanded.

"I'm going to kiss you until you talk to me," he said matter-of-factly. "Not that I'm not going to enjoy every minute of it either."

"Not that—" she began in bewilderment, a bubble of panic rising inside her. Dignity and sanity seemed to be things from her past.

He reached for her with one sinewy arm, and Sara stiffened. She couldn't afford to let herself become involved with Joe. He was unlike anyone she had met before, and that alone made him dangerous. Couple that with the fact that he could probably charm Carol out of her money with ease, and he was one very explosive package.

But even that burst of caution wasn't enough as Joe drew her toward him, and she stared into his handsome, open face. She was on the point of letting him kiss her again and caution be damned. He ran a finger down her nose, and his voice came out a raspy whisper. "Sara, I don't want to push you into anything too fast. I mean, what with your husband's death and everything. But I'll be damned if I can stop myself."

It was the words "husband's death and everything" that did it. Suddenly she felt as if she'd been drenched with ice water. After what had happened with John she must be all kinds of fool to let this good-looking farmer seduce her in his pickup truck. My God, he'd laugh over this later, while he was counting her money!

"Joe," she said firmly, drawing back and out of his embrace.

"I know. I'm sorry I rushed you."

"Please don't say anything until I'm finished. There's something that needs to be straightened out here. It's only fair that you get compensation for housing and feeding Carol and Eddie. I don't begrudge you that. But we need to settle on a figure."

"What?" His voice trailed off in obvious bafflement.

"We can have their car towed to a garage. I'll pick up the bill for that, too. Since they seem to like it here—"

"Since they seem to *like* it here," he repeated with sarcastic emphasis. "What the hell are you talking about, Sara?"

"What I'm saying is that I don't mind your making

some money on what you've done for them. I'll reimburse you for your time and expenses. Motel rates—whatever we agree on."

She darted a glance at him, noticing the narrowing of his eyes, the grim line of his mouth. A tractor trailer sped past them, its wake buffeting them like a gust of wind preceding a storm. A long silence hung over them as she stared out the windshield.

"My God, you think I want money, don't you?" he demanded thickly.

"There's nothing wrong with that," she said quickly. "I realize you've done a lot for Carol and Eddie."

"And always with payment in the back of my mind," he suggested darkly. "I may be a rural bumpkin at heart, lady," he said with icy deliberation, "but I'm no kid. I'm thirty-eight. And I know when people think I'm after their money, no matter how they sugar-coat the accusation."

He nearly snapped off the ignition key with the energy he expended in starting the truck. A split second later they were back on the road, Joe's large, rough hands throttling the steering wheel.

"I've met cynical women in my time, but you take the prize, Sara. Blue ribbon in mistrust." His laugh was dry. "An Iowa farmer trying to charm a little cash from the pretty lady and her sister. Now that *is* a good one."

"I don't need this," Sara said wearily.

"Well, I sure as hell have no use for it myself. I busted my damn knees, half the bones in my body, and Dad's peace of mind to be a baseball player. Hell, I was so tired of eating plastic food in restaurants and having a hotel maid make my bed in the morning that I could've kissed the ground when I finally got back to Iowa for good. But by God, I made enough money on my own to buy back the land we had to sell years before, when times were hard. And to buy some new equipment, to boot." Fierce pride and a lingering sadness warred in his eyes, and Sara felt her heart catch when she looked at him. "Mom died, and Dad had to do it alone for a while. But as soon as I could, I got back home. And now I run the farm and Dad runs the newspaper, and we help each other out whenever we can. We've done it on our own, and I damned well don't need your money to keep doing it."

This wasn't at all what she'd expected. She thought she'd made the offer with dignity. She thought she'd given him a graceful way to take the sum he deserved and still understand it was all he'd get. But apparently she'd badly misjudged him. This big man with the rough hands was obviously stung by her offer. After galloping in to rescue Carol and Eddie, had she fallen off her white steed?

"I didn't drive all the way to Iowa to insult you," she said warily. "But it's been my experience that nothing's free in life. Everybody wants something."

"Well, I'm not making a pretty little speech just to be coy before I blush and accept your damn money." He maneuvered the truck between the culverts on either side of the drive leading to the farmhouse, and Sara caught a glimpse of the Twin Oaks sign as the truck picked up speed and roared up the lane. "When your sister and her husband ran their car off the road, they needed help. Maybe I should have demanded to see their American Express card before I hooked the tractor to their car. Or maybe I should have asked for a peek at their bank book before Dad drove them to the hospital. But money didn't seem important at the moment. And when they needed a place to stay, I didn't count the silverware, either."

He slammed on the brakes in front of the house. With a muttered growl he jerked open the truck door and jumped down, slamming the door behind him as though he'd prefer to rip it from its frame. He took two steps toward the house, then stopped and turned to glower at her. "I hope you made your bed this morning," he snapped. "I'd hate to have to charge you for maid service." He dug his heels into the ground as he strode toward the house.

Sara slowly slid down in the seat and closed her eyes. She felt like a character in a Saturday morning kids' cartoon—*The Lone Ranger Meets Sir Galahad*. So how was she supposed to ride away in a cloud of dust when she'd just botched the whole rescue mission?

# Chapter Four

SARA KEPT ONE eye on the kitchen window while she mixed a batch of springerle cookies. She hadn't seen hide nor hair of Joe since he'd stalked off, leaving her sitting in the truck. Hide nor hair? Already she was beginning to think like a farmer.

She'd been phrasing apologies ever since, but if Joe didn't show up soon she was going to forget her carefully rehearsed words. *I'm really sorry. I didn't mean to hurt your feelings.* That would do for a start.

Her heart skipped a beat as his tall figure suddenly appeared from behind a barn, striding in the general direction of an oversize garage. She attributed her pounding pulse to the hartshorn—its pungent smell filled the kitchen.

Sara opened the oven to check the first batch of cookies, and a licorice-like aroma of anise wafted out. Using a corner of her apron as a pot holder, she pulled out the cookie sheet and transferred the cookies to a rack on the counter. Thoughtfully, she wiped her sticky hands on the apron she'd found in a drawer and tied around her waist. What she needed was a peace offering.

Five minutes later she was heading purposefully toward the garage, a napkin with four hot cookies cradled in her hands. The garage was obviously old, she noted, from the looks of peeling paint on the outside to the packed dirt floor inside. Wild grapevines had crept up one end of the garage and now spilled over the roof as though determined to devour the whole building.

Inside, it was dim and dank, filled with rusty pieces of machinery, a stack of old tires, and several oil barrels with dirty rags draped over their rims. A pile of rags lay on the floor. Smack in the middle of all this stood Carol's red Camaro, a bare light bulb swinging in a slow arc above it, casting deep moving shadows. A pair of jean-covered legs protruded from under the car.

"Is that a tarantula crawling up your leg?" she began conversationally.

The leg jerked slightly, then stilled with obvious iron discipline. A big hand stretched out from under the car and picked the insect up, tossing it aside. "That's a daddy longlegs, not a tarantula," grumbled the voice under the car.

"Could have fooled me. I thought he was going to walk off with your leg."

"It takes at least twenty-five of them to do that."

"Oh. Well, I'll let you know if I see an army of them marching toward you under a flag."

This was going to be harder than she'd thought.

"What's that smell?" he demanded. She heard a wrench clank.

Sara sniffed. "I don't know. It's probably gasoline or oil, although I wouldn't rule out year-old dirty socks."

"No, the food. You brought some with you."

"As a matter of fact, I made you some cookies, as an apology."

The legs inched out from under the car, followed by flat stomach, torso, and finally that handsome face, the blond hair disheveled and spattered with oil. He wiped his hands and arms on a gray rag as he stood up, and Sara watched with fascination as he managed to smear more oil on himself.

"You must have the nose of a bloodhound," she marveled. "I sure couldn't smell cookies in here. And I'm holding them."

He stopped oiling himself and poked the rag back into his pocket, scrutinizing her solemnly. "Actually, I snuck a look into the kitchen half an hour ago, so I knew you were baking. When you came out here, I figured you had some cookies with you." He still hadn't smiled, but she got the impression he wasn't furious with her anymore.

"Well, here," she said, holding out the napkin. She took a deep breath. "A very contrite apology goes with these."

"You don't have to explain," he said grudgingly, taking the cookies with definite enthusiasm and immediately stuffing one into his mouth.

"No, I was awful. I hurt your feelings, and I was totally ungrateful for what you've done for Carol and Eddie."

In the ensuing silence, he said, "You forgot something."

"What?" she asked, sighing.

He swallowed the last of a cookie. "You refused to wear the sneakers I gave you today." He popped another cookie into his mouth.

Sara shifted her weight and rolled one corner of the apron around her finger. "Am I banished from Iowa?" she asked tentatively.

He considered and swallowed. "Naw. That's just if you dent my pickup. Some things are sacred to a farmer."

From the corner of her eye, Sara saw something move on the garage floor, and took a wary step backward. "Those rags are alive," she murmured.

Joe glanced in the direction of the rags and gave a soft whistle. The rags pulled themselves together and turned into a low-slung dog that lumbered to its feet, mounted on enormous paws. The ears swung ponderously close to the ground as the dog made a laborious path to Joe. He reached down and scratched behind the dog's ears, and it yawned appreciatively, tail wagging in a slow rhythm. "This is Stafford," he said. "He's a basset hound. Never was much of a hunting dog though. He was trailing a raccoon once, and a rabbit jumped out of a bush. Scared old Staff half to death. He turned tail and ran back to me."

Sara smiled in spite of herself. "Poor Staff," she murmured, stooping down and patting the dog's head. He turned soulful eyes on her and yawned again.

"He won't go anywhere near a rabbit now," Joe said. "He likes bugs, though. These all the cookies you brought?"

Sara nodded. "I've got more in the oven." She stood up and found herself almost nose to chest with Joe. Slowly she raised her head and looked into his face. He was still chewing, but his blue eyes were dark with an expression that had nothing to do with cookies. Sara felt a sweetly warm immobilization stealing through her limbs. She wanted to melt against him and have those hard muscles support her. "I really am sorry about what I said, Joe," she murmured, staring up at him.

"Does that mean you're not leaving?" he asked softly, his voice deep and husky as a rumble of distant thunder riding a summer night.

Sara took a deep breath. "Not right away. If I can stay."

"I'd like you to stay here. I'd like that a lot." He smiled then, and she felt as if the sun had suddenly beamed on her, making her blood pound with languid heat. He dabbed at her nose with the rag from his pocket. "You've got flour all over your face," he said. Grinning, he pulled away the rag. "Now you've got oil on you, too. Do me a favor."

"What?" She barely heard her own voice. She didn't seem able to focus on anything but the sheer overpowering presence of him. He was so tall, so rawboned—so absolutely gorgeous. His eyes were more soulful than Stafford's.

"Go put on my mom's sneakers. You're going to ruin your feet."

Sara sighed and leaned away from him, breaking the magnetic field that seemed to draw her ever closer. "Okay," she agreed. "Well, I'd better get back to the cookies before they burn." She dragged herself away and started for the yard.

"Sara?" he called softly behind her.

She stopped and looked back at him.

"Your husband—John?—what was he like?"

She didn't need to ask him why he wanted to know. He was no dumb farm boy. Joe seemed more attuned to her—after even this short space of time—than anyone else she'd known.

Joe was watching her face, his own partially hidden in the deep shadows of the garage. "Did he let you down somehow?"

"Yes, he did." She gave him a small shrug and took a step backward. "I'd better check those cookies."

He didn't stop her this time, and she found herself trotting toward the kitchen. As soon as she slid the last cookie onto the cooling rack, she took the sneakers from the corner where she'd left them that morning and slipped them on. They were comfortable and soothing—like Joe.

\* \* \*

They sat on the porch again that evening after dinner, Joe, his dad, Carol, Eddie, and Sara. And Miss Mary Morehead, a wiry woman in her eighties who refused to leave the crumbling farmhouse a mile down the road despite pleas and threats from distant relatives who stood to inherit the land, and friends who feared the house would fall in around her ears any day. Miss Mary, as everyone called her, sat in the Dancys' old wicker rocker, her birdlike legs stretched out straight in front of her, displaying support hose and orthopedic shoes. Gnarled fingers interlaced in her lap, resting on a white dress splashed liberally with purple flowers. Occasionally she turned her head to send a stream of chewing tobacco into the spittoon at her feet.

Miss Mary had raised six children, half of them hers, half of them castoffs from other families, and she had taught grade school for fifty years, while her husband farmed. When he died ten years ago, Miss Mary dug in her heels as relatives offered to take her in.

"Like salmon swimming upstream to spawn," Miss Mary grumbled as a rusted yellow pickup truck went past on the road. She nodded toward the truck. "My grandson. No doubt he's headed to see that new little girl friend of his. An idiot if ever I saw one."

Joe laughed, and Miss Mary shook a finger at him. "You never brought home any prizes either, Joseph. Sara's the only real prospect I've seen cross this threshold, and I think she's too good for you." Joe grinned and propped his feet on the railing. Sara felt her face grow hot. "All those ninnies I've seen you with, Joe, why, you could throw them all in a big kettle and still not have enough brains for a puppy dog."

"No intelligent female wants an Iowa farm boy, Miss Mary," Joe said, teasing her. "They all want baseball players."

"Posh! I think you enjoyed the attention from all those airheads. They told you how great you were." Joe was laughing, head tilted back, hands clasped over his flat belly. "You just go ahead and laugh," Miss Mary warned him. "I'll dance at your wedding yet." She spit generously into the spittoon.

They all fell into a comfortable silence, listening to the chirping of crickets. "Hear that?" Joe asked Sara as a faint rumbling reached them. "That's a car crossing the old bridge over the creek. McFeeters Bridge. It was named for Miss Mary's family. They settled right there by the creek when her grandfather came here from Ireland. It's the local necking spot today. What would Grandpa think of that now, Miss Mary?"

"I think he'd be all for it," she said. "He liked his drink and his women. You'll have to give Sara a tour of the bridge. Preferably on a moonlit, romantic night," she added.

"I don't know about that," Joe said slowly, and Sara recognized his teasing voice. "I think Sara's too ornery to go with me. But maybe she'd change her mind if I promise to bring Staff along as our chaperon."

"Joseph Dancy," Miss Mary said slowly, "you darn well deserve to be a bachelor."

"Yes, Miss Mary, I reckon so."

"Miss Mary's been showing me how to crochet," Carol interrupted. "I started a muffler for Eddie."

"Every color under the sun is in that thing," Eddie commented, laughing when Carol thumped his knee. "I'll look like a walking rainbow."

"Just for that, I'll wear it myself," she said.

"Oh, please, Carol, don't take back my muffler," Eddie pleaded in mock contrition. "How will I keep my neck warm this winter? Joe says Iowa winters are brutal. You don't want me to freeze my brain, do you?"

"You already did, a long time ago, sport," Carol informed him.

"You're planning to stay here a while, then?" Sara

asked casually. From the corner of her eye she saw Joe turn to look at her.

"We love it here," Carol said enthusiastically. "And you do, too, don't you, Sara?"

"It's very pretty country," Sara said hesitantly.

"I can hardly wait for you to see the newspaper," Carol went on, apparently not perceiving her sister's lack of enthusiasm. "And once you're settled in, maybe Miss Mary can teach you to crochet, too."

"I'm afraid I've got ten untrainable thumbs," Sara said graciously.

"Besides that, I'm reserving you exclusively for cookie baking," Joe threw in. "I know where your talents lie."

"You're all assuming I'll move lock, stock, and barrel to Iowa," Sara said. "I just stopped here to see how Carol and Eddie are doing." She refused to look at Joe.

"But you don't have anything to do before you go to Europe," Carol said. "Why go back to an empty apartment? You need to get away and get over John."

"I can't just move in here," Sara protested.

"Not a reason in the world why not," J.D. said from the shadows of the porch. "We have the room. And we'd all like to have you stay for as long as you can. Besides, Joe says I always burn the cookies."

"You do," Joe confirmed. "Hell, I save them and use them as charcoal briquettes in the barbecue grill."

Sara looked around the row of faces as if she'd find the answer she wanted there. Half of her—the half that had offered Joe money—told her to pack Carol and Eddie into their broken-down car and tow them back to Chicago. The other half—and this was a persuasive half, because it was the one that had caught fire under Joe's kiss—was whispering something quite different in her ear . . . If she liked Iowa and if, despite all protests to the contrary, she liked Joe . . . And if Carol and Eddie were staying, there was no better way to keep an eye on them.

She could make sure they didn't get into any trouble, and do it without insulting Joe. She still didn't understand him, didn't comprehend why a man would shelter two strangers without asking anything in return. All right—a small part of her suspected he *did* have some ulterior motive. But if he did, she would ferret it out soon enough if she stayed.

"All right," she said quietly. "I guess you have a house-guest."

This time she did look at Joe, and his gaze pulled her inexorably deeper into the spell of the summer evening. He was regarding her with thoughtful, shadowy eyes, and she was sure he suspected it wasn't just love of Iowa or a fondness for his pickup truck that had convinced her to remain.

Carol, Eddie, and J.D. were happily congratulating themselves on Sara's decision, and Miss Mary was advising Joe to get Sara to the bridge with all possible speed. "Otherwise, she's going to figure out you're no great catch."

Smiling stiffly and thanking them, Sara stood. Explaining she was tired and wanted to go to bed, she closed the screen door softly behind her, letting her eyes adjust to the darkness of the house. Only a patch of moonlight filtered through the windows to illuminate the wood floor and staircase. She stopped at the stairs, running a hand over the spinet that sat in a recessed corner just under the banister. On impulse, she lifted the hinged seat of the piano bench and pulled out a piece of sheet music. She flipped on a small lamp and saw what she had chosen. "Yesterday." She smiled ruefully.

Sliding onto the bench, she depressed the soft pedal and lightly touched the keys. The piano was a little out of tune, but the melody whispered softly, echoing in the alcove. She played it all the way through, unable to stop thinking of John. This was the song they had danced to at their wedding reception—"their" song. It seemed fitting that they had chosen a song that spoke of the past, not the present or the future. How was it possible to be so wrong about a person? To love a man without really knowing him? She didn't think she'd ever get over John's betrayal. If her husband could do this to her, then anyone could.

"Do you know 'Stardust'?"

"I didn't hear you come in," Sara said. Joe leaned on the banister, chin propped on his folded arms.

"That piano hasn't been played in years."

"Do you play?"

Joe shook his head. "I took some lessons as a kid, but the teacher gave up. She said my hands were too big. Mom taught me to play "Chopsticks," and she'd play the chords. We used to sit here together, and she'd laugh and muss my hair."

Sara patted the piano bench. "I think I remember those chords. Want to play a duet?"

"Yes, indeed," he said solemnly.

She couldn't seem to stop watching him walk toward her, the sinewy fluidity of his hips, the intensity of his eyes. He sat down, his thigh touching hers, and Sara felt a warmth grow in her loins and spread through her blood like a fever. She had sat this close to John in candlelit restaurants, but she'd never experienced the rush of desire she felt when Joe's jean-covered leg brushed hers. *Don't think about that, Sara.* She forced the thought from her mind and smiled as Joe put his index fingers on the keys, giving her a crooked grin. "Maestro?" he said.

Sara made a show of arching her hands, shaking her fingers loosely and delicately as she positioned them on the keys an octave below his.

He started, and Sara joined in, playing the chord accompaniment, trying to follow Joe's choppy rhythm. They were both laughing as they raced to the finish, Joe's big fingers tripping across the keys. Impulsively, Sara reached up and "mussed" his hair. It was soft and silky, and a shiver of awareness ran up her arm like an electric current. It was only natural for him to turn toward her, his blue eyes filled with laughter and glowing heat. Her hand stilled, but it remained in his hair, loath to leave such inviting softness. At that moment the laughter between them turned to something else, the way rainy sky turns to rainbow when the sun suddenly shines. She felt his hand span the small of her back, gentle pressure urging her closer. She strained toward him, a sigh catching in her throat as his other hand cradled the nape of her neck, chasing a sensuous wave of pleasure down her spine.

That fleeting thought of John dissolved in the air like insubstantial smoke as all the sensations associated with Joe assailed her—his clean scent, the corn-yellow color of his hair, his callused hands. At the moment those hands were moving slowly over her back, reducing Sara's insides to warm honey.

*"What's that spot under the piano bench?" J.D. would ask the next morning.*

*"Oh, that's just Sara," Joe would say. "Darnedest thing. She melted last night."*

Time undulated over itself like waves on a shore or corn stalks bending in the wind, and the next thing Sara knew, Joe was kissing her. A wild, unfettered response rose within her. Her fingers tightened in his hair, pulling him even closer. Some invisible, spidery thread seemed to connect them, so that she felt her pounding pulse follow the trail of his hands over her ribs, thumbs caressing beneath her breasts, lifting them gently. His fingers sought her nipples and stroked them with such unerring sensuality that her head fell back in a soundless gasp, his mouth still clinging to hers in a deepening kiss. His mustache made her upper lip tingle.

His lips left hers to forge a trail of fiery response along her jawline and to her throat where he breathed her name hoarsely.

"Joe," she answered softly, hardly recognizing her own voice.

Someone laughed outside on the porch, and a rocker creaked. Sara's eyes flew open. She tried to marshal her senses, acutely aware of where she was.

She heard the slow smile in Joe's voice. "It's okay, honey. We're not committing any crime, at least not under Iowa law. Can't speak for Chicago."

*A crime.* "He didn't commit any crime in the strict, legal sense," the lawyer had said. "But morally he's guilty as hell." Well, Sara wouldn't be victimized twice. Her father had taught her that one mistake was bad enough; repeating it was unforgivable, not to mention stupid. She was staying here to protect Carol and Eddie, Sara reminded herself, not to let Joe Dancy cloud her judgment with his irresistible lovemaking...

She pushed against him and straightened up, painfully aware of the flush creeping up her throat. She stared at Joe, trying to read the expressions flitting across his handsome features.

"I sure as hell would like to know what makes you tick, Sara Scott," he said softly. "You're as soft and sweet as a kitten one minute, and the next you act like I suggested you pose nude for a cattle feed ad. I don't know what I'm doing that ruffles your fur, but if you feel like telling me, I'm more than willing to listen."

Sara averted her eyes. She had no explanations to offer. She knew how easily she could fall into his bed, as compliant as the kitten he'd likened her to, but she wasn't about to make that mistake. Undoubtedly Joe Dancy had had a lot of women in his bed—some kittens, some tigers—and undoubtedly he had enjoyed them all and made them feel appreciated. He was the kind of man who made a woman feel special. In his own way John had been like that. A charmer, who could make Sara feel very good about being a woman—when he wanted to.

"I'm a bit short on answers tonight," she said at last, sparing him a brief smile. "I think I'll go to bed."

She knew he watched her go up the stairs, and she lingered at the top, listening to his slow rendition of "Chopsticks." His hands might be too big, but he sure as hell could make a simple little song sound sad.

# Chapter Five

SARA WAS HAVING a not unpleasant dream. In it a man who might have been either John or Joe—this part was unclear—was telling her how much he wanted her, and he was exploring her body with intimate caresses. The man was talking to her in deep, tender tones, raining praises on her, and she lapped it up like a kitten in the cream crock.

She could feel his hands stroke her hair, and she could hear his voice. "Come on, honey. Wake up." No, she didn't want to do that. The dream was far too pleasant.

"Sara," the voice called. "Time to wake up."

"I'm sorry," she muttered groggily, "but I don't want to."

He was laughing now. "Come on, honey." The hand stroked her hair, and she pulled the sheet up to her nose.

Her eyes opened a slit, took in the darkness of the room, and, satisfied that it was the middle of the night, snapped shut again.

He was insistent; she'd give him that. Now he was gently shaking her shoulder. "Now, sweetheart, are you going to make me get a bucket of cold water?"

"I'll kill you," came her icy reply.

"That's what I like," he said cheerfully, "a woman who wakes up all bubbly and full of sunshine."

"Buy a rooster if you want sunshine," she informed him. "If you haven't noticed, there is a definite absence of brightness outside. Most people, Dancy, have enough sense to realize that means it's night."

"Now, Sara, come on. We're going fishing."

She sat up slowly, blinking and clutching the sheet around her neck. "You know, I could have sworn you just said we're going fishing."

He grinned enthusiastically. His hair was still mussed from bed, and despite her sleepy state she couldn't help noticing that he looked darned rugged in those jeans and a red flannel shirt that made his hair look like the sunshine that was so sadly lacking at this hour.

"I told you about the trout up north, remember? Well, I'm going to introduce you to a few."

"Couldn't you just invite them over for coffee?"

"We'll do that, too, sweetheart," he said, humoring her. "Time to get dressed. Here." He held out the package she'd seen him carrying from the general store, then tossed it onto the bed. "No more pretty skirts. I don't want the trout distracted."

Apparently he was through badgering her, because he stood up and backed to the door, smiling. "I'll pack some sandwiches," he promised.

"Take your time," she called, but he had already started that tuneless humming as he left the room. Sara stared balefully at the package, wondering what he'd picked up for her. Knowing Joe, there was probably a pair of rubberized hip boots in it. Or sneakers. Or maybe some of his old shirts. With Joe you never knew.

She tucked the sheet under her arms and unrolled the brown paper bag, gingerly poking in a hand and feeling around. She pulled out a pair of jeans and, murmuring in surprise, dumped the contents on the bed. Another pair of jeans, three checked cotton shirts, and white socks. Sara stared at the clothes. He'd planned on her staying from the day they'd driven to town. Sara raked a hand through her tousled hair. She knew she'd be conceding something if she dressed in these clothes, and she'd be meeting him on his own turf. But at this hour she didn't much care about concessions. She dressed in the red checked shirt and a pair of jeans, grimacing as she put on white socks and then the old sneakers. So this was how one dressed for trout! She considered pinning her hair up, then just ran a brush through it instead.

Sara stifled a yawn. She was so tired! And chilly. She lifted her robe from the foot of the bed and wrapped it around herself, then lay back down for just a minute.

"You deserve some rest," she assured herself groggily as her head hit the pillow.

Sara stretched lazily. Mmmmm. That felt so good. She curled her toes. Absolutely delicious. A tendril of hair was delicately stroking her chin, not quite tickling. Mmmm. A tendril of hair? Sara's eyes flew open.

Joe was sitting on the edge of the bed staring at her, one large hand playing with her hair. "You're just not a morning person, are you?" he demanded.

"What gave me away, Sherlock Holmes?"

His eyes moved down her throat and over her torso. Her silk and cashmere robe was a champagne shade, far too delicate in contrast with the jeans and shirt. She saw a look cross his face, and it momentarily confused her. Almost disdainfully, his eyes hardened. So Joe had something against cashmere and silk? She didn't have time to dwell on it, because he picked up the baseball cap lying on the bed and lightly tapped her head with it. "Breakfast. Downstairs." She gave him a mock salute as he exited her room for the second time.

She could hear deep voices as she made her way down the stairs and toward the light in the kitchen. She stopped in the doorway, blinking in the brightness. Joe and J.D. were sitting at the kitchen table with a stranger.

"Sara," Joe said, jumping up as he noticed her in the doorway. "I want you to meet a friend of mine."

"Bailey Stevens," the gangly redhead at the table said, grinning as he stood up and advanced to Sara, holding out his hand. His handshake was firm, and she noticed with amusement that he directed his light blue eyes, not as compelling as Joe's darker ones, in an unhurried assessment of her. "Pleased to meet you," Bailey said, giving her a smile that Sara guessed was calculated to start a bonfire under her libido. It didn't work, but Sara had to admire his confidence.

Joe was watching Bailey with wary speculation, and Sara got the impression he wasn't exactly thrilled with Bailey's attempt to charm her. Joe cleared his throat. "Bailey and I played ball together, Triple A and at Baltimore. He was a fair fielder but a lousy hitter. He almost had a homer one day when a freak windstorm came through Memorial Stadium just as he hit the ball. Wind died, though, before the ball got out of the park."

"That's real funny, Dancy," Bailey said with a grin. "But it just so happens I could outhit you any day of the week."

"Maybe if you had one of my church league boys pitching to you," Joe ribbed him in a lazy drawl. He pulled a red sweat shirt from behind his back and said to Sara, "Here, this'll keep you warm." He began to pull it over her head, smoothing back her hair. Sara couldn't help noticing that Joe was making the gesture as proprietary as possible. She glanced at Bailey as her head came through the neck opening and saw his eyes narrow in understanding. Message received.

Sara frowned and moved away from Joe, shrugging the sweat shirt on the rest of the way herself. She didn't belong to Joe Dancy or anyone else, she told herself sternly.

When she scowled at Joe, she saw him grinning at her as if he'd read her mind. He shoved a thermos into her hands, along with something wrapped in wax paper.

"What's this?" Sara asked.

"Breakfast. Come on. Let's go."

"Have a good time," J.D. called after them. "And don't tell Sara a bunch of tall tales." He winked at her while Joe and Bailey raucously protested their innocent intentions.

It was the pickup truck again. Sara despaired of ever riding in true comfort. Joe loaded tackle boxes and rods into the back, tunelessly humming all the while. He got in, and she found herself sandwiched between the two large men, jostled back and forth as Joe shifted gears. She must have dozed lightly, because she woke up suddenly when the truck hit a bump, and found her head resting on Joe's shoulder. She straightened hurriedly, and he pretended not to notice. Sara fooled with the thermos on her lap and poured herself a half cup of coffee. It was strong and bitter. She unwrapped the wax paper and eyed a sandwich of some kind. A tentative sniff didn't tell her anything, so she took a bite. Ketchup? Gingerly she lifted the top slice of bread and tried some field identification. "What is this?" she finally asked.

"A Dancy Special," Joe said cheerfully. "It's great."

"Did this come out of a cookbook or is it your own invention?" She chewed hesitantly, trying to guess at the mixture of flavors.

"Old family tradition. Dad used to make one for me every morning. Two eggs scrambled with chopped bologna and Tabasco sauce. Spread the bread with a little cream cheese and jam."

"What kind of jam?" she asked.

"Peach."

Sara coughed and managed to swallow a bite anyway. "Egg McMuffin it isn't."

Bailey was laughing, and Sara guessed he was no stranger to Dancy breakfasts.

The truck pulled up to a curb at the first stop light in town, by a drugstore, and Bailey hopped out and got in back. Joe explained that they were picking up another friend, and Sara peered curiously at the deserted sidewalk, where streetlights still cast a soft glow. A lone mongrel dog ambled around the corner, and Sara tossed out a piece of her breakfast sandwich. The dog ran over eagerly, snatched up the morsel, then let it drop from his mouth. He tried it again, and again he spit it out. With a wary glance up at Sara, he trotted on up the street.

"Dancy Special," Sara hissed triumphantly. "And that dog's no gourmet."

"Staff likes them," he countered. She didn't have an answer to that, other than to point out that Staff was also afraid of rabbits.

A moment later the door of an apartment over the drugstore opened, and a portly man with florid face and contrasting white hair hurried out, carrying a tackle box and rod and reel. He and Bailey exchanged a few words, and Bailey tossed the newcomer a pack of gum.

"Rudy Wernowski," Joe called, "meet Sara Scott."

Rudy grunted a hello and shook Sara's hand after stowing his gear in the back with Bailey. "And don't go messing with none of my flies," he called out to Bailey as he got in the cab next to Sara.

Sara smiled. She couldn't imagine anyone willingly messing with a bunch of flies. Still sleepy, she rested her head against the back of the seat, closing her eyes, idly listening to the men talk. From what she gathered, Rudy was a retired umpire. Joe was telling him about Bailey dropping in unexpectedly the night before. Apparently this was normal behavior for him.

"Broke again?" Rudy grunted.

"Yeah," Joe said quietly. "Got in some trouble over in Missouri. Fight in a bar or something."

"How long you think he'll hang around this time?"

She sensed Joe's shrug. "No idea. He was by here last winter and stayed two weeks. I gave him a couple hundred bucks before he left, and I'm sure Dad slipped him a fifty."

Rudy sighed deeply. "Hell, he knows you'll always take him in. Always did."

Joe didn't answer for a minute. "He's a friend."

"Yeah, yeah. Aren't they all? That's your trouble, Joe. Too good-hearted. Even when you were playin' ball, you were like that. Wouldn't spike a man or take him out so as to hurt him."

"I never saw the need," Joe said with more than a trace of stubbornness.

"And any guy needed a little money to tide him over always touched you for it, didn't he?"

"They always paid me back."

"Hah! That's a crock if I ever heard one."

When Joe answered, Sara could tell he was smiling. "Well, most of the time. Hell, Rudy, what's your point?"

"Bailey. What he needs is a solid right hook to his stupid jaw."

"Well, I've given him one or two of those in my time. Only straightened him up temporarily."

"Yeah, that's Bailey." Rudy sighed deeply, and Sara felt his weight shift as he settled down farther in the seat. "I never knew one boy could find so much trouble without hardly trying."

Sara learned from the rest of the conversation that Bailey frequently dropped in at Twin Oaks, never announced, often arriving in the middle of the night. Usually he was broke, and often he had been in trouble of one kind or another. Other names were mentioned, and

Sara gathered that the farm was more or less a free hotel for Joe's many and varied friends. She pretended to be asleep when Rudy asked Joe if Sara was one of his old friends.

"Sara came out here from Chicago to check up on her sister Carol. Carol and her husband are staying at the place."

"She'll probably take off in a few days, then," Rudy said around a yawn. "Give her an autograph and a look at your World Series ring, and she'll go home and tell everyone about the baseball star she met."

Joe gave a noncommittal grunt, and Sara could imagine his eyes giving her a quick sweep.

"Despite your handsome mug," Rudy said, yawning again, "you sure as hell don't know anything about women. They like the fast life and the glamour that goes with being a star. You never did take advantage of that, son. You can have any woman you want just by flashing your smile and your news clippings. Shoot, there's nothing wrong with using a little bait."

"Not so sure I want to keep what I catch with that."

Rudy laughed. "No need to keep it. Just have a little fun. Hell, boy, I've watched you operate over the years, and believe me, you need some pointers. You don't take a nice, pretty little lady who comes to see a baseball hero and show her the cow pies in your pasture. You don't say, 'Isn't this the most beautiful corn you've ever seen?' And you don't ask her if she'd like to milk a cow."

Sara could sense Joe grinning. "Damn, Rudy, I thought that kind of stuff turned women on."

Rudy gave an exasperated sign. "Stubborn farmer, Joe. That's all you are." In a suspicious tone he added, "Hey, you never brought a woman fishing before, now that I think back."

Joe laughed. His arm came around Sara and gently tugged her until her head rested on his shoulder. She felt him shift his position until she was nestled against him.

Rudy leaned out the window to yell something back at Bailey, and Joe laughed, his hand brushing her thigh.

She actually did fall asleep, and Joe had to nudge her awake as the truck came to a stop. Sara sat up and blinked, then realized she was still cradled against Joe, his body warmth generating more than a little heat in her bloodstream. He was grinning down at her, and as she stared back owlishly, he ran a long finger down her nose and said, "Come on, Sara. Let's catch us some trout."

Rudy was already standing by the truck, stretching and complaining to Bailey that he'd let his tackle box jiggle around during the ride.

Joe tugged her out of the truck on his side, pulling her against him as he helped her down. They were both slightly breathless as he held her, his hands spanning her waist. Her breasts just grazed his chest, and his eyes turned smoky as she stared at him. The playfulness quickly faded from their faces, and Sara swallowed hard. She wanted him to kiss her right there, take her in his arms and hold her tight, and she didn't care if Rudy and Bailey and all the trout in Iowa were watching. But he didn't. Slowly he lowered her to her feet and released his hold on her. Sara couldn't stop staring at him, not even when he turned to the truck to get their gear.

Joe led them all to a small log cabin office near a running stream. There he got them fixed up with fishing licenses. Grinning crookedly, he pinned Sara's to her sweat shirt.

She glanced around when they came outside, taking in the bank of the stream lined with rough-barked trees, thick leaves forming a canopy of shade. Fishermen were lined up along the bank, leaning against the trees or working over their rods and reels. Nobody was fishing.

"What's the deal?" Sara whispered to Joe. "Aren't the trout here yet?"

"We can't start until the whistle blows at five o'clock."

Sara trundled after him, Rudy and Bailey bringing up

the rear. She'd never heard of fish who punched a time clock. She wondered if they got overtime for nibbling on bait after sundown. The cold morning air rose from the ground like a mist, and dew was so thick on the grass that it looked like fresh rain.

Joe scouted up and down the bank until he found a spot that met his high standards, and while Rudy and Bailey began setting up their equipment like seasoned veterans, Joe explained the rudiments to Sara. "This is the reel," he said, his voice slow and patient.

"So I gathered," she said. "And the fishies are in the stream."

"Now, don't be cute. I'm giving you valuable information here." He took off his cap and placed it on her head sideways, pulling the brim down over one eye. "The fancier the lure the better the trout like it. I have a great collection of flies that Dad and I tied over the winter."

Imagining a miniature jail cell containing houseflies, their legs bound with thread, Sara stared in macabre fascination at the tackle box. When he opened it, she saw only brightly colored constructs of rubber, metal, and feathers. Joe magnanimously let her select her own lure, and she pointed to a long purple worm made of rubber. Joe sighed as though he was exhausting his patience working with a rank amateur, but he fastened the lure on her line. What followed was a brief lesson in casting. Since the whistle hadn't yet blown, this was accomplished in pantomime, and Sara reveled in exaggerating the movements while Joe stood watching with his arms crossed, one eyebrow raised skeptically.

"Think you've got it?" he asked.

"No problem, Joe," she said, yawning widely.

He muttered something, then set about prepping his own rod and reel. They all stood poised on the bank with their fishing rods like so many soldiers waiting for a commander's order to fire. When a shrill whistle blew, the simultaneous plop of lures was heard all up and down the bank. But not at Sara's spot. Her long backswing, learned on a Chicago tennis court, had landed her line in the limb of a nearby tree.

"Are we having fun yet?" she dared to ask Joe as he stood on tiptoe untangling her line.

Tersely he informed her no, not yet. He moved close behind her, his body pressed against the length of hers, and she had a difficult time concentrating as he guided her arm back and then snapped it forward, sending the line softly whooshing over the water. "Then reel it in slowly," he whispered next to her ear. "Trout like movement."

Sara wasn't averse to movement herself, especially the way his hips brushed seductively against hers. She felt her breath quicken, and she handled the rod clumsily, causing Joe to have to help her again. This time his hand trailed softly down her arm on the follow-through, and she swallowed convulsively.

"Sara?" he whispered against her ear, and she turned to see him smiling wickedly. "Now we're having fun," he said.

Sara straightened with dignity and menaced him with the rod. "I'll take it from here," she informed him, and he moved away, grinning. She sent him sideways glances the whole morning, loving the fluid movement of his hips as he cast the line, and the way the muscles of his arms knotted as he reeled it in.

Rudy caught the first fish, and everyone rushed over to watch as Bailey scooped it out of the water with a net. Bailey took time to hand-roll a cigarette before he went back to his own line. A minute later he laid the rod on the bank and ambled back toward the truck with a slow shuffle. Joe glanced at him, then set his own rod on the bank and followed. When Sara looked over her shoulder she saw both men sitting under a tree by the parking area. She had the feeling that Joe was trying to straighten Bailey out again, without resorting to a right hook.

It seemed to her that men formed a secret fraternity, pledged to take care of their own. John had joined several service organizations and an athletic club where he played racquetball. Whenever he and Sara argued, which had happened often during the last year of their marriage, he would call one of his buddies. They would go out for a drink, or to some other place that was apparently off limits to Sara. John would come home late, alcohol on his breath, and Sara would hear him in the den doing paperwork until after midnight. She wondered if he had ever told his buddies about his manipulations of her trust fund . . .

After one more glance back at Joe and Bailey, Sara squared her shoulders and cast her line again. She was reeling it in, sighing and wondering just how long she was expected to stand here and do this, when her line dipped violently, then went taut. Sara was too excited to speak, and she tugged on the rod until she remembered she was supposed to reel in the trout. "Joe!" she shouted, as she dug in her heels and leaned back. Before she turned her full attention to the fish, she caught a glimpse of Rudy farther down the bank. He was staring at her, slack-jawed.

"Here, fish," Sara coaxed, edging down the bank to get a better heel hold. The bank was slick with wet grass and mud, and she felt her feet sliding out from under her. "Joe!" she called desperately. She held the rod tightly in one hand, her other flailing madly. Both feet went skittering, and Sara sat down hard on the bank and down into the stream on her posterior. She came to rest in icy water up to her waist. Tenaciously she clung to the rod.

She heard a chuckle behind her, and the next instant Joe was wading into the stream. "If you laugh," she threatened.

"I would never laugh at someone trying to land the first trout of her fishing career," he said so solemnly that for a moment she wanted to hug him. But that would require her to release the rod, and she was not about to let the trout get away! Not after all the aggravation it had caused her.

Joe sized up the situation and instructed her to reel in her trout while he got the net. A moment later he was scooping the fish out of the stream and she was grinning up at him from her decidedly wet sitting position. "A beauty," Joe pronounced, holding the fish up for the crowd to see.

The men seemed more interested in the sight of Sara plunked down in the stream, and she pushed herself to her feet. Water ran in gushing rivulets from her jeans as she trudged to the bank, carrying her fishing rod. Joe came back to clasp her hand and help her to shore. Then he surprised her by swinging her up in his arms and holding her close as he climbed the bank. They were both wet, and her damp hair clung to both their faces, but Joe just grinned, looking as proud as though he'd just caught the biggest fish in the whole state of Iowa.

Bailey was standing at the top of the bank, thumbs hooked in his belt, rocking on his heels as he surveyed them. "Caught a good one, did you, Joe?" he asked as he chewed on a blade of grass.

Joe still held tightly to Sara. "A real beauty," he said.

Bailey looked at Sara thoughtfully, then pulled the grass blade from his mouth to make his judgment. "Yep. I'd say you reeled in a right smart catch. Wouldn't mind one like that myself."

"Then find your own stream to fish in," Joe growled.

"And here I just wanted some good advice," Bailey complained, grinning as he walked away.

"Joe," Sara said gently. "You can set me down now."

"Well, I'd like to, Sara, but there's one small problem."

"What's that?"

"When you carry a rod, you should secure the hook. Right now yours is lodged in the seat of my jeans."

"You mean—" she began, and then she started to giggle. The giggle turned into laughter. "Looks like I caught more than a trout," she teased him.

"Want to have me stuffed and mounted? Now, come on. Unhook me." He slid her to the ground, and she sidled around behind him, surveying the damage while he held her rod, the line arcing over his shoulder.

The hook was imbedded in the denim, and she worked at it with her fingers. "Hold still," she muttered. "Now Rudy's staring."

"Well, hell, I guess so. You're taking your time messing with the back of my jeans."

"Hush. That sounds awful. And stop squirming. Now that man in the red shirt is starting to watch." The hook was slippery and hard to disengage.

"Honey, I can't stand here like this much longer, smiling and nodding at a whole bankful of fishermen who think I'm the strangest sight they've seen in a month."

"Well, this is no picnic for me either. I'm drenched! And I'm going to rip your pants in a minute." She lowered her voice as several more fishermen turned to throw curious looks over their shoulders. "I don't know why you brought me trout fishing in the first place." She gave a yank on the hook, but it was still stuck.

"Ow!" he complained. "Those pants are connected to my body. All that tugging isn't doing much good to my . . . uh, my legs."

"Cutting off circulation to your brain, no doubt," she retorted, but the situation was turning her fingers to thumbs.

She muttered under her breath, and he said, "What?"

"I like my trout baked and stuffed and lying on a bed of rice on a china plate," she grumbled, "not splashing

around on the end of a hook and smelling like the city
dump."

"You can't tell me you didn't have a great time catching that trout," he countered. "I saw the gleam in your
big green eyes, Sara Scott." He lowered his voice to a
teasing whisper. "Or was that gleam for me?"

"Oh, you . . . you . . ." She searched wildly for the
proper words while more fishermen stopped casting to
observe. "You farmer!" she finished irritably, jerking the
hook free with an audible tear of fabric. "And you wear
red underwear!" she threw in as a bonus.

"Sara!" He feigned shock. "These are my lucky red
undershorts."

As the flush started up her neck, she snatched her
fishing rod from him and strode off toward the stream,
the hook bouncing in the air. She heard Joe chuckle
behind her, but she wouldn't acknowledge it. Every fish-
erman on the bank was now staring openly, and Bailey
was doubled over in laughter.

The thing was, Joe was right. She'd thoroughly enjoyed catching that trout, and she'd had an even better
time being carried. And he knew it!

She tried to maintain her detached attitude for the rest
of the day, despite Joe's sidelong glances of amusement
and the lingering smiles he sent her way as they ate
sandwiches for lunch. And despite her resolve, on the
ride home, she fell asleep between Joe and Rudy. Dimly
she could hear Bailey singing, his mournful baritone
drifting in from the back of the truck. The truck bounced,
and Sara's head fell to one side, finding its way somehow
to Joe's shoulder. She half woke later and realized his
arm was around her, but she didn't move, and she could
have sworn he kissed the top of her head.

"You sure sleep a lot," he told her, grinning, as the
truck came to a halt at the farmhouse.

"You smile too much," she rejoined, trying to stifle

a yawn as he helped her down from the truck. It was night again. Sara thought with longing of the bed Joe had dragged her from in the middle of last night.

Bailey was still singing. Tilting his head up to the dark sky, he looked like a dog baying at the moon. Now Rudy joined him, looping a friendly arm around his shoulders, his tenor decidedly off key. Joe laughed and took up the song—"I'm So Lonesome I Could Cry"— and Sara joined in, too. The crazy thought crossed her mind that she was going to miss Joe Dancy's brand of insanity when she was off in Europe.

# Chapter Six

SARA SLEPT SO deeply that when she woke up the next morning she wasn't quite sure where she was. When she saw Joe's sweat shirt draped over the back of the chair she remembered the fishing expedition, and a sleepy smile tugged at the corners of her mouth. J.D. had been waiting up for them with a camera, insisting that Sara pose with the three trout she'd caught. Joe had stood with his arm around her shoulders, his grin as wide as hers, and when the flashbulb went off he had hollered, *"Trout!"* so loudly that Carol and Eddie came stumbling from bed. Then everybody was telling fish stories at once, and Joe was explaining why the seat of his jeans was ripped.

Sara put on jeans again, and pulled on the honey-colored T-shirt that was among the clothes Joe had bought her. Her slightly wavy hair was beginning to look entirely too untamed after a whole day free from the confines of pins, but Sara didn't stop to worry about it.

When she got downstairs, Carol, Eddie, and J.D. were just leaving, and her sister kissed her cheek, commenting that Sara had acquired a glow.

"Probably sunburn," Sara said uncomfortably, trying not to look at Joe.

"Well, you look great. Farm life agrees with you." Carol danced out the door after Eddie, calling over her shoulder. "Got to get to the salt mines. One of J.D.'s reporters quit yesterday."

"A regular country girl," Joe teased her when the door closed. "Bloom of the fields in your cheeks. The kiss of the sun in your hair. The wind's caress in—"

"All right, all right," She poured herself a cup of coffee and sat down. "So where's everyone else?"

"Rudy took the newspaper out to the front porch, and promptly fell asleep there. Bailey's still in bed. He was up prowling around until four this morning, so I imagine he'll sleep till afternoon." Joe sat down at the table with a cup of coffee and a couple of Sara's cookies and gestured toward the doughnuts. She took one and nibbled at the chocolate icing.

"Does Bailey have any family?" she asked idly.

"His family's a big part of his problem. His dad pushed him into baseball from the time he was a kid, and now that his playing days are over, I guess he feels he can't measure up in his dad's eyes."

"I take it he's not married?"

"He was once." Joe's voice changed tone, became more tense. "The old story. She got tired of him when he wasn't a hero on the field anymore. Last I heard she'd found someone else with an up-and-coming career."

"What about you?" she asked bluntly.

Joe shifted in his chair. "I suppose I'm a little more suspicious than Bailey was. Seems like every woman I meet wants a piece of yesterday's glamour but none of today's hard work." He took a drink of coffee and abruptly changed the subject. "Now, Rudy's a lonely man, too. His wife died several years ago, and he never had kids. Dad and I bring him out to the farm every chance we get."

It seemed that Joe and his dad took in anyone who wandered past their door. And what did they get in return? she wondered curiously. What made them open their arms to friends and strangers alike?

"Was yesterday the first time you went fishing?" he asked, and Sara said yes without thinking.

"No," she corrected herself slowly. "I almost forgot. My uncle took Carol and me fishing in his lake when we were kids. All we caught were sunnies." She stared down into her coffee, frowning. It hadn't been much fun, she remembered. To say the least.

"Was that in Chicago?" he asked.

"No. He lived on a little horse farm in Kentucky." She had been thirteen at the time, Carol five. Uncle Dick and Aunt Becky had invited them to spend part of the summer there. He had taken them fishing two or three times, always fidgeting, as though he didn't relish the task—and it did seem to Sara that it was a task for him. She would hear him talking to Becky at night when she and Carol lay in the twin beds on the second floor. She couldn't make out the words, but the cadence and tone were recognizable—worry.

Dick had driven the girls back home after two weeks, talking with forced joviality all the way. In Chicago, he asked the girls' father if he could speak to him alone. When Dick emerged from the closed den an hour later he was ashen. Refusing an invitation to spend the night, he grabbed his hat and left immediately for home, his gait suddenly old and stiff. At dinner Sara's father said to her mother in a cold voice, "You never get something for nothing. When your brother invited them, I told you he was after something." He quieted down only after a sharp glance from his wife and a nod toward the girls.

Sara guessed what had happened a month later when Dick and Becky lost their home. Her mother finally admitted that Dick had asked his brother-in-law for money, and he had been refused. At the time Sara felt sad for her aunt and uncle, but also angry that they had used her and Carol.

"You hate fishing, right?" It was Joe's voice, a note of such unhappiness in it that she was jerked violently out of the past and smack into Joe's kitchen, her uncle's plea for money still ringing in her head. "I made you do something you don't like."

She shook her head quickly. "No, I really enjoyed yesterday." When his face relaxed in a grin she added, "Except for that part about getting out of bed when the chickens were asleep. But speaking of *making* me do something, Joe Dancy—"

"Uh-oh. I should have kept my big mouth shut."

She was about to let him have it with both barrels—for talking her into making him cookies and wearing jeans, and for getting her half drowned in a stream full of trout, for heaven's sake. She was about to enlighten him on her exact opinion of men who treated women like that, but the image of her extricating her fishing hook from Joe's jeans came back so clearly that she laughed instead. At least Joe had the grace to look confused—and relieved.

"Your pants," she coughed out between gasps of laughter. "Your red underwear." Fresh laughter. Tears were beginning to stream from her eyes.

"I'm glad that amuses you," he said, working to sound indignant, but his efforts not to smile failed miserably. "Bailey gave me those undershorts as a joke, and I caught a whole passel of fish wearing them. They always guarantee me a good catch."

She was still laughing, and he was grinning at her

across the kitchen table. And then the way the sunlight glanced off his unruly blond hair—making it look like a dandelion in full glory—made the laughter die slowly in her throat. His eyes were dancing with deviltry and that look that could always make Sara weak in the knees. Her gaze came to rest on his mouth, full and firm and, oh, so delicious. How could any man who wore red underwear and took her trout fishing, of all things, have such a devastating effect on her? He stood and moved slowly around the table.

She let him draw her to her feet, leaning into him and reveling in the sudden acceleration of her pulse and the way her breath became shallow and quick. The creak of a chair on the front porch stopped the slow descent of his head to hers, and they both glanced through the kitchen toward the living room and the front door beyond.

"Come on," Joe said softly, his eyes caressing her again. "Let's get out of here."

"What about Bailey and Rudy?" she asked.

"They deserve to be left alone with each other. Besides, I've been promising you a tour."

And a tour it was. Joe found an extra cap somewhere, red like his own, and so they left the house in matching jeans, shirts, sneakers, and now caps. "At least you look like a proper farmer," he informed Sara.

"Joe, the finest agriculture college in the world wouldn't turn me into a farmer," she retorted.

All that got her was her cap pulled down over her eyes.

He showed her the pastures, the cornfields, the barns, the grape arbor where he'd hit her instead of Dunbar, and finally the two giant oak trees in front of the house that had given the farm its name.

"Come here," he said with boyish enthusiasm, tugging her up a grassy rise on the west side of the house. "Come here," he repeated, his voice husky. He pulled her in front of him and crossed his arms around her waist, pulling her back against him. "Now, isn't that about the most beautiful sight you've ever seen in your life?" he demanded, his chin resting on her hair.

She had to admit it was breathtaking, or maybe that was just the effect of his nearness. Spread out below was a verdant valley dotted with Hereford cattle grazing next to a stream.

"It's downright bucolic," she teased.

"City slicker," he whispered into her ear, and a shiver chased through her as he nibbled on her earlobe.

"What are those purple flowers?" she asked in a strained voice. Actually it was the first question that came to mind, and she latched on to it to mask the sudden loss of equilibrium. She was glad it was a reasonable question . . . Her state of mind made coherent thought difficult.

"Venus looking glass," he said.

"They sure attract the bees," she persisted, as he softly bit her ear.

With a grin that said he was well aware of her discomfort, he took her hand again and pulled her back toward the house.

"Is this the See-the-Iowa-Farm-in-Ten-Days tour?" she asked, stumbling after him, trying to keep up with his giant strides.

"On your right is the noted Notre Dame Cathedral," he intoned as he marched on, not slowing his pace, "and on your left a quick glimpse of the Swiss Alps. Behind us is a breathtaking view of the Roman Coliseum, and of course in front of us is the world famous Dancy camper."

They had been walking—no, running, she amended— around the house and behind the grape arbor, and now they stood before a small camper-trailer parked near the garage where Joe had been working on Carol's car. As campers went, it was not impressive. It had a standard metal body, dented here and there, with a hitch in front. One tiny window adorned the side, and Sara could see white ruffled curtains.

"I've fixed it up a bit," Joe said apologetically, "but it needs a lot more work." He opened the door and showed her inside.

Sara blinked as her eyes adjusted to the dim light. She turned awkwardly, trying not to bump into anything as she looked around. She heard Joe's step behind her, and then they were pressed hip to hip. To her immediate left was a minuscule sink and at right angles to that a small bed. A cupboard faced the sink.

"Bathroom," Joe explained, pointing to a door in the opposite wall. To the right of that was a little table with benches built into three walls.

Sara could see that even one person would knock knees with himself sitting there.

"I like it," she said honestly.

Joe beamed. "Dad bought it when he and Mom were first married. Because of the farm and the newspaper, they couldn't take long vacations. Instead, they went to local camping grounds in this. And when they were too busy to do even that, they'd sometimes spend the night in the camper, right here on the farm." He nodded toward the bed. "Family legend has it that I was conceived there."

"I love this rural folklore," Sara said lightly, somewhat disconcerted by his intimate disclosure. This was another thing that threw her—Joe Dancy was so casual and open about everything. There seemed to be no artifice about him, no attempt at concealment. Sara was at a loss to handle that.

"I've got to tighten down the table," Joe said, apparently choosing to overlook her discomfort. "And I need to replace the shelves in the cabinets. Plumbing could use some fixing too."

A wren started chirping outside the camper, and Sara remembered glimpsing a small birdhouse on a limb of a redbud tree. The camper filled with a comfortable silence, like warm sunshine. A fly droned in the window, and the breeze came up to ruffle the corn. *What did he want?* Sara was at a loss to explain Joe Dancy. On the surface he was a kind man, someone who valued his friends and his life here on the farm. His wants were few or else he managed to hide those he had. She had never met anyone like him, and she was still warily appraising him. What complicated matters was his enormous—and very physical—appeal. She knew why all those women came to see the baseball hero. But she didn't understand why they weren't equally enchanted with the farmer. She was. Lord, she was trying to resist it, but she realized it was a losing battle. The man fascinated her. He was like a drug in her bloodstream, and right at this moment she was feeling an undeniable urge to lean back against him to let the moment lead her where she knew it could— to that little bed in the corner.

"My husband and I talked about seeing the country," she said hesitantly, each word seeming to leave her painfully. "A motor home seems a good way to do it." She didn't know what made her say it, but something about Joe and about his pride in this little, worn-out camper touched some memory she'd hidden since John's death. She searched scenes of the past. "I hadn't thought about that in a while."

He waited.

"I don't know what happened," she said, finally facing the fact that things had gone wrong in her marriage, long before John's death. "It seemed to wear John down, trying to make money. He stopped talking about trips. He seemed obsessed with the kind of power that money could give him." She took a deep breath. Joe's hands were gently stroking her arms, soothing away the tension she was fighting. "We stopped going to the lake for picnics. Time was money and money was everything."

"Maybe John was just trying to be a success in your eyes," Joe suggested softly.

"It's possible," she murmured. "Sad for him, wasn't it?"

Joe didn't answer. The wren was singing again, and

she listened, giving herself over to the incredibly gentle touch of his rough hands.

"We said some awful things to each other during the last year of our marriage," she confided. "It still hurts to think about it. He accused me of holding my inheritance over his head when I questioned him about our investments." She closed her eyes tightly, then opened them again, staring at the small rip in the paneling on the opposite wall. "As it turned out, he was losing more and more money. I didn't even know it. He would have lost the whole inheritance. And he couldn't even tell me..."

"Sara." Joe's voice promised what she needed at that moment—comfort, understanding, someone to lean on. She heard more in that single utterance of her name than she'd heard in all the words John had tossed her way. She closed her eyes, trying to see John's face one more time, to remember how it had looked to her before things went bad. But instead of her husband she saw Joe, blue eyes warm and filled with promise.

She turned swiftly in his light embrace and buried her head against his chest. His hands came up to her hair, stroking away the pain, and his husky voice whispered, "I know, Sara, I know."

He smelled outdoorsy and male, and she inhaled deep drafts of the clean scent of his shirt, rubbing her cheek against its softness.

Unconsciously her hands sought the firmness of his back, caressing the hard muscles, winding their way up to his rough-textured hair. Her face tilted up to look into his, seeking those beautiful blue eyes, and he rewarded her search with a heart-stopping hunger in his gaze, a need that seemed to spring from deep within him. She realized with a pang that there had never been this naked need between herself and John. Always, there was too much caution, too much that was guarded between them. Never any letting go. Not like now, when she felt that if Joe didn't kiss her she would go crazy...

But he did kiss her. And she responded so hungrily, pulling his head down to hers, parting her lips and welcoming the invasion of his tongue that was so demanding, so compelling...

"Sara." He groaned, half pulling himself away from her. "Sara, I don't think I can take this, honey. I've wanted you since I first set eyes on you. I don't mean to hurt you, Sara. If you won't let me carry you over to that bed, then you'd better tell me so right now." His voice dropped to a gravelly whisper. "I need you, but if you're not ready—"

"Yes, Joe. I want you, too."

It was impossible, after all, to scoop up someone in that tiny camper, and Joe ended up pulling her backwards, his arms pressed tightly around her, his mouth never leaving hers. He laid her gently on the bed, his head raised sufficiently to take a long look into her eyes. "Sara, you know I'm not playing around, don't you, honey?"

"I know, Joe." She did. But she didn't care at this moment. All that mattered was that she needed him as she'd never needed another human being in her life.

Her answer released his passion, and he knelt beside her on the floor, raining tender kisses over her face and throat. "You're so beautiful," he told her, a note of awe in his voice, and Sara felt his words sear her very soul. His hands, so large and used to hard work, praised her in their own way, his touch arousing her body as he worshiped it.

His fingers sought to learn everything about her, each minute response, until he unerringly stroked the most sensitive areas of her body. In each touch he gave her, in each gentle caress, she could sense his pleasure in pleasing her. She treasured that gift he presented her, taking his caresses and praise-words to her heart, because no one had given to her so freely before.

His hands were too big to manage her buttons easily, and he gave her an apologetic smile when she had to help. "I'm going to buy you shirts with snaps from now on," he teased her huskily. "Hell, I'm frustrated enough half the time just looking at you, not being able to touch you."

She felt frustrated, too, when he bent his head to her naked torso, his tongue moving in slow circles from her waist to her breasts, his mouth tightening on her nipple, sucking it to taut hardness. She arched up to meet his moist touch, loving the tension mounting inside her.

Joe unfastened her belt and slid her jeans off with a spurt of energy that made her laugh. He buried his face against her belly, rubbing his jaw over her hip bones, lips sliding sensuously around her pelvis while she moaned his name. The friction of his light beard and his mustache against her skin produced a wild excitement in her loins. When she didn't think she could stand it anymore, she pulled his head back to hers.

"Let me undress you," she whispered, and his off-center smile of hungry delight was her reward. She sat up, making long work of it, because he couldn't seem to take his eyes off her—or his hands. When his shirt was on the floor he stood up, and she pressed her mouth to his flat stomach, her hands splayed on his hips, aching with the need to have him touch her again. She unzipped his jeans and pulled them down, then pulled him down on the bed with her—a tight squeeze at best—and tried to tug his jeans all the way off.

"Honey," he laughed from his position half on top of her and half scrunched against the wall, "I usually take my shoes off first."

She swatted him playfully, and they were both laughing and tussling like children until they accomplished their objective, which was to render them both naked. This done, the laughter faded comfortably, lingering only in Joe's blue eyes. He rolled over, pulling her on top of

him, sliding her up his body until her breasts were poised
over his mouth. He licked one and then the other, leaving
Sara moaning and writhing. That inflamed his own desire, and play swiftly turned to hungry lovemaking. He
rolled her onto her back, and his leg nudged her thighs
open, his rough hair rasping against her more tender flesh
and making her pulse pound in unbearable excitement.
He took care to stroke kisses and tiny-nibbles from her
throat to her stomach until both were breathless and
flushed.

She had to touch him, had to feel his hard body with
her fingers, to prove to herself that he was real. Sara ran
her hand over his chest and down his stomach and then
to his legs. He groaned and buried his head against her
neck. He entered her quickly, and his thrusts produced
a new burst of ecstatic desire. He prolonged the pleasure,
stopping to tease her by nibbling on her throat and earlobe.

"Joe," she breathed raggedly. Feverish excitement
made her move beneath him, and that proved more than
his control could handle. Whispering softly how beautiful
she was, Joe increased the rhythm of his thrusts until
Sara arched sharply against him, her hair fanning behind
her in a mahogany cascade. She was flying in Joe's
embrace, soaring above the cornfields, riding the breeze.
Pleasure exploded in a burst of sunshine and hot shivers.
She clung to Joe, staring into a beautiful blue sky that,
she slowly realized, was really Joe's eyes, tender and
caring and moving over her face lovingly.

"I love you," he murmured so softly against her ear
that she was sure a moment later, as she drifted off to
sleep, that she had dreamed it after all.

# Chapter Seven

SARA STRETCHED LANGUIDLY, feeling wonderful. For a sleepy instant, she didn't remember why. She only knew she must have been dreaming of heaven. It was when her foot encountered a hairy leg that she remembered. Heaven was right in this narrow bed with her: over six feet of gorgeous blond farmer.

She turned her head and saw him watching her from hooded eyes, a mile-wide grin lighting up his face. One arm was looped possessively around her, and he showed no intention of turning her loose. He wiggled his toes against the soles of her feet and continued to grin.

"You look like the cat that got the cream," she teased.

"Sara, honey, I *did* get the cream. I don't think I can wipe this smile off my face for at least a year."

She turned in his arms, already feeling a rising tide

of desire as she looked into his eyes and saw how much he still wanted her. Oh, Lord, no one had ever made her feel like this before! She felt a brief pang when the voice of reason insisted on its note of censure: *You don't know this man.* But even reason couldn't compete with a lazy summer afternoon in Iowa and a man who had just shown her paradise.

"This little camper sure can go places," she said. "I could have sworn we made a trip to the moon and stars."

He pulled her tightly against him, his lips nibbling insistently at her ear and throat.

"Hey, Joe, where the hell are you?"

It was Bailey's voice, right outside the camper, and Joe groaned. Sara snatched at the single blanket at the foot of the bed and tried to unfold it and wrap it around them. To her discomfort Joe chuckled.

"What's so funny?" she hissed. "For Pete's sake, get some clothes on."

She was plucking his clothes from the floor, tossing them at him, and trying to fend off his hands, which were surrendering to the temptation presented by her naked body lying crosswise over him. "He'll hear you," she pleaded as Joe continued to chuckle.

Sara began to dress with breakneck speed. One of her buttons flew across the room, hitting the floor with a loud snap, and she cursed under her breath.

Joe pulled on his jeans. "Honey, I didn't know you knew words like that," he said in mock surprise.

"Brace yourself," she said. "You're going to hear a few more."

"You really are worried about Bailey finding out what we're up to, aren't you?" he said, seeming surprised at the discovery.

"Of course I am."

He tucked in his shirt. "Are you embarrassed about us?"

"No, I . . . " She stopped tying her sneaker to look up at him. She wasn't sure why it bothered her that someone might find out she'd slept with Joe. She stared at him helplessly. "There hasn't been anyone since John," she began lamely, embarrassed by her admission. After all, hadn't she heard tales of his many women?

Some of the tension left his shoulders. "Hell, Sara, I'm sorry. I wasn't thinking about your feelings. I'm acting stupid as all get-out. Listen, sweetheart. Until you want us to, we won't do this again. I don't want you to feel—hell." He cupped her face in his big hands and gave her a quick kiss on the lips.

"You find him yet?" came a voice from outside, Rudy's voice.

"Naw, he must be out in one of the pastures." Bailey again.

Joe gave Sara a last, warm smile and squared his shoulders, then opened the door. "You two bozos looking for me?" he growled, stretching his frame across the doorway so they couldn't see inside.

"Hell, yes," Bailey said. "The Chicago game's on TV in a few minutes. You coming or not?"

"Well, I'm not sure," Joe said. "I've got some disking to do. On about twenty acres."

"Come on," Rudy urged. "You got all summer to disk. We're talking the Cubs against St. Louis."

Joe laughed. "All right. You go on, and I'll be there in a few minutes."

"Say, I haven't seen the camper in a while," Bailey said with a burst of enthusiasm. "You done any more work on it?"

"No, not a lick," Joe said with a trace of impatience. Bailey had taken a step toward the door, but Joe continued to block his view as well as his path.

"What's wrong with you, Joe?" Bailey demanded. "What are you hiding in—" He broke off suddenly, and

Sara heard him chuckle. "You got a harem in there or something, Joe? Or maybe just one special someone, right?"

"Bailey," Joe said in a warning voice.

"Yessir," Bailey said. "Joe's been fixing things up in the camper. Come on, Rudy. I know when we're not wanted." He moved away, chuckling.

Joe watched them before he turned to Sara with a self-conscious grin. "If it's the last thing I do, I'm going to find wives for those two."

She folded the blanket and placed it carefully at the foot of the bed, berating herself for being so silly; she definitely didn't want to leave the camper just yet. "Is that severe enough punishment?" she asked lightly.

"Hell, no. Bailey wouldn't know what to do with a decent woman anyway. But I imagine marriage might soften up their rough spots a bit and maybe get them off my backs so I could enjoy a little peace and quiet." Sara turned from her perfunctory bed-making and saw him watching her, arms crossed, blue eyes clouding with an emotion she didn't recognize. She had just made love to the man, and she still didn't understand him. She had only come to understand John after his death—his need to prove himself, his frustrations, his constant need for approval. Joe wasn't like that at all. At least she didn't think he was. But what kind of man *was* he? And why, when those blue eyes studied her, did she feel, deep down, that she understood him on some elemental level? She was startled by the depth of her feeling for him, and a momentary panic assailed her. She couldn't let herself love a man she hardly knew.

"Are you okay, Sara?" he asked. "You aren't sorry, are you?"

"No, of course not," she said swiftly, wondering if she was sorry after all. Sorry she had started to care about this man. "We ought to get back to the house before someone else comes looking for us."

She started to move past him, but his arm came out and caught her around the waist, and a flash fire of desire erupted in her veins, spreading to secret places that remembered his touch and craved it. She let herself lean into him for just a moment, pressing her eyes closed with the aching need to be in his bed again.

"You're not sorry?" he repeated, fingers stroking the small of her back.

She shook her head, but didn't meet his eyes. "Come on." She sensed his eyes straying to her as they walked to the house, and she avoided his scrutiny by focusing on the Venus looking glass in the meadows. Everything looked brighter and fresher in Iowa—the sky, the cornfields, the flowers—and she wondered if that same luster was causing her to see Joe in a golden light. In her experience, there was more illusion than reality in the world.

Rudy was in the recliner in the living room, cracking his knuckles impatiently, when Joe and Sara came in. Bailey sat cross-legged on the floor, a plate of scrambled eggs balanced on his lap, an open can of beer on the rug. The two men had cajoled Stafford into joining them, and now he sprawled beside them, floppy ears spread-eagled, his nose pressed against the cold beer can.

"So what did you do," Bailey demanded around a mouthful of eggs, "take the scenic route?"

"Who planned your brunch menu," Joe rejoined, "Staff?"

"Pipe down!" Rudy leaned forward in the chair, shushing them. "Two runners on and one out."

"Two outs to go, right?" Sara asked brightly, and Joe shook his head tolerantly.

He dropped two fat pillows on the floor in front of the couch and lowered himself to one, spreading his bent knees and beckoning to Sara. He tugged her into the crook of his legs and pressed her head to his chest. "Now this hitter coming up has a lousy record against their pitcher. My guess is he'll bunt."

Sara's body reacted as though he were whispering tender endearments—not baseball strategy—into her ear. "Bunt?" she repeated blankly.

But before Joe could explain, something momentous must have happened, because Rudy was screaming, "Pitchout!" and Bailey was bellowing, "The runners are going!" and Joe was shouting, "Safe! A double steal!"

"What happened?" Sara asked, directing her question to the dog, since no one else was paying the slightest attention to her.

All three men started explaining at once, and Sara looked from one to the other. Before any could conclude his commentary, the predicted bunt occurred. There was a wild flurry of activity at the spot where the catcher stood. Sara listened to the three arguing about whether or not the runner was safe and decided baseball was a lot more complicated than she'd been led to believe.

"So how long to halftime?" she asked.

A chorus of groans greeted her question.

The game lasted three hours. Lunch turned into an uncivilized affair of ham sandwiches and potato chips and beer. By the end of the ninth inning, Sara was feeling a certain leadenness in her posterior and a decided urge to hiccup from the quantity of food she'd consumed. Watching baseball seemed to involve a lot of calories and a corresponding amount of stress—brought on in part by disagreements between the team managers, umpires, and pitchers, not to mention the three men seated beside her. But they seemed thoroughly delighted with the whole affair, and Sara wondered at this intense camaraderie that seemed to emerge out of sports.

Joe stretched and grabbed Sara's hand. "Come on," he urged, pulling her to her feet. "Tour's not over."

"Goin' to show Sara the camper again?" Bailey drawled as Joe tugged Sara toward the door.

"Thought you had disking to do, Joe," Rudy chimed in.

Even Staff turned disbelieving eyes on them.

Joe swore under his breath and stalked toward the door. Staff apparently knew Joe deserved his loyalty, because he lumbered to his feet and followed.

Sara turned on Joe the moment they were outside. "If you have disking to do . . . " she began, but he stopped her with a shake of his head.

"The disking can wait another day. And Bailey and Rudy know how to feed and water the livestock. Hell, they live here most of the time. Come on." He opened the truck door.

Sara couldn't decide which was worse—Jumping Jones and his rancid cigar or Stafford the basset hound, whose personal fragrance was not enhanced by the July heat. But Staff was enamored of her, and he spent the ride in the truck with his head stretched across her lap, soulful eyes staring up at her.

"He has an eye for the ladies," Joe explained. "Flirts shamelessly."

"They say dogs are like their owners," Sara observed.

"Couldn't be," Joe teased her. "I've never run from a rabbit in my life."

"What do you run from, other than starry-eyed women who come looking for autographs?" she asked suddenly, not really sure she wanted to know the answer. She knew enough about Joe to be sure he would give her a candid answer.

"I don't know that I run *from* things anymore," he said reflectively. "I used to when I was playing ball. I'd try to avoid the sportswriters after the games because I hated having to answer those questions about how it felt making this play or that. I mean, it's not easy to avoid sounding like a pompous ass when somebody says, 'Hey, Joe, tell me what you were thinking when you hit that triple in the eighth.' And if I told the truth and said I was just praying I didn't strike out, since my contract was coming up for renewal, the guy wouldn't believe me." He pulled the truck to the side of the road in front of a school and turned to look at her. "I can sure tell you what I run *to*, if you're interested in that."

She nodded, absently stroking Staff's ears.

"This place," he said, gesturing with a short nod. "Iowa, my farm, my dad, summer evenings on the porch, working on my camper. People have told me I'm crazy for not wanting more, but I don't think there *is* more. There's *different*, but not more."

"Playing baseball was different, wasn't it?" she asked.

"Yes, it was. I love the game. And I won't lie and say I hated having the chance to play it professionally. It's a rare privilege and believe me, I know how lucky I was. But it isn't forever. It's a game for young men, and boys with stars in their eyes. What I've got here in Iowa is something you can grow old with. A life that lets you feel good about yourself." He gave her a swift smile. "Thank you for not telling me I'm crazy to love the farm."

This was all so different from Chicago! And Joe was so different from any man she'd known before. So different from John . . .

Sara sighed. She could certainly understand Joe's deep attachment to this place. It had *home* written all over it. And an aching longing had risen in Sara's throat. What was wrong with her? A couple of days in Iowa and she was sprouting roots. Just like a potato! She was city, she told herself. She loved to work—on a newspaper, not a farm—and she liked to eat from fine china in restaurants and walk on concrete in high heels, and she liked men in three-piece suits with stylish haircuts. So why the hell wasn't she homesick for any of those things?

"Anyone who's as much in love with his life as you are, Joe Dancy, can't be crazy."

He regarded her silently for a long moment. "I don't think you're going to find what you're looking for in Europe, Sara," he said at last, softly.

When she tried to read his expression, she saw a haunting depth in his eyes, like skies that stretched to the ends of the universe. She stared into those eyes, trying to figure out his secrets of happiness and love of life, but she was too confused. Emotion got in her way. An emotion that belonged to Joe, and which had no place in the heart of a woman who had been hurt by a man she loved! Too many defenses were nailed in place. And she refused to recognize the answering emotion she saw in Joe's face...

"I'm not looking for anything in Europe," she said. "I just need to get away. To relax a little."

"You can do that right here."

"Oh, sure," she said, reverting to a teasing tone, hoping to change the tenor of the conversation. "I hate to tell you this, Joe, but the heartland of America tour you've given me, complete with battling trout, is *not* relaxing."

His mouth curved into a grin, but in his solemn eyes she saw that he understood her ploy. Then his expression relaxed. "What? No kidding? Well, hey, I'll have to change that. Nothing but rest and relaxation for the Chicago lady. Okay?"

"Good. Now I can sleep until sunup."

"You're welcome to take an afternoon nap in the camper anytime you want," he said innocently. "I realize that the farmhouse isn't exactly—private." And then—his voice grew serious. "If you're not ready for this, Sara, why, I can wait. It'll be hard, don't mistake me. But I give you my word. We're kind of clannish out here, and people tend to know other people's business. If you're not ready for that—"

Warmth curled in Sara's belly at the thought of his concern; it spread inexorably to every corner of her body.

"I think I'd better steer clear of the camper for now," she said carefully. She didn't know what Joe expected of her, what reward he wanted for all those caresses and kisses so tenderly bestowed. As Sara's father had taught her, there had to be a reward. Even John had expected money in return for love...

"Sara," Joe said quietly, and his eyes seemed to look right through her. "I know you're still angry with your husband, but I'm not him, sweetheart."

"I'm not angry," she protested, a little undone that he had, indeed, read her mind.

Joe shrugged. "Okay." He stared out the window, and Sara stared down at her hands, and Staff stared at both of them in turn.

Sara broke the silence first. "So where are we?" she demanded, looking curiously at the school where he'd parked.

"Right now I'd say we're at an impasse. And I respect that, Sara. I won't pressure you—" Catching her glance, he held up his hands and said, "Okay. Literally speaking, we're in front of the high school that had the dubious honor of graduating me." He hopped out and opened her door, taking her hand and pulling her up the sidewalk to the front door. The old Joe, lighthearted and teasing, was back, cupping her face in his hands as he peered beyond her into a window. "Come here and look at this!" he said. Sara leaned closer and peered gingerly into an empty classroom. "Mrs. Elrod's science class," Joe announced. "It was here I dissected Susie Peterson's frog for her."

"Didn't Mrs. Elrod frown on that?"

"Not after Susie threw up on the first frog."

"In my class it was Randy Hartman passing out over planaria."

"Really?"

She nodded solemnly. "I heard he became an orthodontist. I guess teeth were more palatable to him."

Joe gave her a window tour of the building, pointing out the classrooms where he had endured all the traumas and triumphs of adolescence, the gym where he had played basketball and subsequently marched to "Pomp and Circumstance" in his cap and gown, and the field behind the school where he had played baseball and won a college scholarship. "And here," he said, looping an arm around her waist and pulling her down next to him on the bottom row of the bleachers with him, "is the scene of my greatest high school triumph, the memorable night when I became a man."

"I don't think I want to hear this," Sara said.

"Sure you do," Joe returned. He straddled the seat and linked his arms around her waist. "Every woman wants to hear a man confess his innermost secrets. Right?"

"You must have some other woman in mind."

Playfully he nipped her earlobe. Why did she have such swift and intense reactions to his every touch? One crook of his finger, and she'd jump into his bed. Pliability, thy name is Sara.

"Her name was Joanne Bentlinger," Joe whispered in her ear. Sara crossed her arms and tried to look bored. "She was blond, pert, and had the figure of a Rock Cornish hen." Sara had to giggle at that, and Joe grinned at her. "She was my first love. The head cheerleader."

"And you were captain of the football team, right?"

"You got it. And right out here behind the bleachers she initiated me into the mysteries of sex one night after a football game."

"Behind the bleachers?" Sara said incredulously.

"Now, it wasn't what you think. The extent of the experience was that Joanne let me unhook her bra. Pretty exciting stuff for a high school kid in those days."

"You call that the mystery of sex?" she demanded.

"Times were different then," he protested in a wounded voice. "I thought I had to marry her after that."

"So why didn't you?"

"We got engaged my second year in college," he said, surprising her with the sudden transition to seriousness apparent in his voice. "I think we might have gotten married if I hadn't signed to play ball." His arms tightened imperceptibly around Sara. "She went with me to spring training, and she fell in love with the idea of being married to a baseball player. In two months she'd decided she'd rather marry a pitcher who had good prospects of being brought up to the majors that year."

"Did she marry him?" Sara dared ask.

"Um-hmm." Joe buried his face in her hair, rubbing his beard-roughened jaw back and forth. "He got called up, hurt his arm, and got sent back down. Then Baltimore decided they wanted to give me a shot in the big time, and Joanne was back. Suddenly I was Mr. Wonderful, the newest catcher on the Baltimore Orioles." He nuzzled the nape of her neck. "Mmmm. You smell good."

"What happened to Joanne?" Sara asked a little breathlessly, trying to ignore her reaction to his touch.

"I told her to go back to her husband where she belonged."

"And the pantyhose heiress?" she asked.

"We went our separate ways by mutual agreement after she got a good look at the farm. I don't think she fancied living so far from real civilization."

"How did you hook up with Bailey?" Sara asked, relieved suddenly at Joe's revelations; she wasn't sure why. Maybe it was his honesty . . . She leaned back not wanting to lose the moment, the sun lulling her into a pleasant lethargy.

"Bailey got called up to the Orioles same year I did. My mom was alive then, and she used to send me giant boxes of cookies, which I shared with Bailey. The poor guy never really knew his own mother, and I think he sort of fell in love with mine. He begged me to take him home with me after the regular season. He became the brother I never had," he added wryly.

"He's a little wild, isn't he?"

"Now there's an understatement." Joe ruffled her hair. "And don't you go feeling sorry for him and baking him cookies. I don't want him to become any more enamored of you than he already is. If he does, I'll have to punch him out. Not that that would slow him down much."

"I'll try to remember that."

"Let's go. You haven't seen the *Weekly Mart* yet."

"A store?" she ventured, letting him draw her to her feet and lead her back to the truck.

"Our newspaper. It's a weekly shopper for the rural area, hence the name."

The newspaper office was on a small street that also sported two taverns, a paperback bookstore with lurid titles in the window, and a dingy bakery whose glass door offered a view of a wedding cake that appeared to have been there for a long time.

*Weekly Mart,* although not an impressive name, was almost too long for the narrow door to the tiny brick building. The *M* in *Mart* had come unfastened, and now hung upside down. Thus the sign read *Weekly Wart*.

"This is a newspaper?" Sara murmured in disbelief as she preceded Joe over the threshold. It looked more like an aged tenement. The wood floor creaked dangerously beneath her feet, and she stood uneasily in the middle of the room, sure she would get oily grime on her fingers if she touched anything. The room was dimly lit by ceiling fixtures, about a third of them operational, which cast a gloomy pall over the room. Two desks dominated the office, one sitting at an odd angle because of a broken leg. The dusty counter was cluttered with papers, half-empty coffee cups, and a single Polaroid camera. A Linotype machine hunched in one corner like an old animal. Nearby stood a device Sara decided must be a headline setter. She was sure there were enough spiders in the corners to stuff a telephone booth.

"I bet Edgar Allan Poe used to work here," she said

uneasily. She had expected a small newspaper, but the
*Weekly Mart*—or *Wart*, as she had already begun to think
of it—truly deserved to be called a rag.

The clatter of the Linotype stopped, and a big woman
in jeans and a T-shirt emblazoned with a sequin butterfly,
whom Sara had somehow failed to notice, came toward
them, smiling. One beefy hand pushed back a strand of
blond hair, most of which was escaping from a ponytail.
The fact that the woman was about sixty did nothing to
soften the impact of the butterfly stretched between pen-
dulous breasts, or the bleached hair.

Joe was grinning. "Sara Scott, I'd like you to meet
Edna Templeton, chief typesetter and head honcho on
the *Weekly Mart*."

Edna pumped Sara's hand enthusiastically. "Everybody calls me Big Ed, honey. Pleased to meet you."

"My pleasure," Sara said faintly. She couldn't imagine
anyone working here willingly.

A clatter on the stairs preceded the appearance of
Carol's head emerging from the stairwell. "Sara!" she
called happily, dashing up the rest of the stairs and rush-
ing at her sister. The handful of papers Carol was clutching landed on the floor, where they were in danger of
being buried by dust balls.

Sara, who had not been hugged much in over a year,
felt in danger of being overcome. Then she caught a
glimpse of the bandage on Carol's hand. Swiftly she held
her sister away to scrutinize her. "What happened?" she
demanded, staring at the bandage.

"Oh, it was nothing," Carol said, waving her hand
casually. "The paper cutter attacked me this morning."
She giggled.

"What?" Sara shook her head. "But that's awful."

"A couple of stitches was all it took," Carol said.
"The doctor's office is just around the corner. Come on.
Let me show you around."

Sara shot Joe an accusing look, but he was leafing through mail on the counter. What the hell was he running here, a sweatshop?

Given the size of the office, the grand tour took all of two minutes. They started in the basement where Eddie and a wiry old man introduced as Jenkins were tinkering with a printing press, enough ink on the two of them to put out a morning and evening edition.

Carol's typewriter in the upstairs office was vintage. One key was missing entirely, but Carol said it was just the *j* and she didn't need it often. But she confessed to having had trouble last week with a feature on a Mexican exchange student named Juan Juarez.

Big Ed proudly showed Sara the Linotype. "Carol and I put the whole paper together last week. Stayed till three A.M. the night before, but we got it done. Didn't we, honey?" She nudged Carol, who nodded and smiled.

Sara picked up a thick issue of the *Weekly Mart* from a desk and thumbed through it incredulously. "You did all this yourselves?"

Big Ed hooked her thumbs, long nails painted mauve, in the waistband of her jeans and rocked back on her sneakers. "Yes'm, we sure did. Had to. Mr. Simms, our features reporter, quit. That left us all in the lurch, but we pulled it off, by golly. Carol pounded out stories till after midnight, and I set them. Joe set the headlines." She pointed to the other machine. "J.D. did the pasting up, and Eddie and Jenkins ran the press."

"Do you have to work like that often?" Sara asked cautiously. Suddenly she was beginning to see why Joe had been so eager to take Carol and Eddie in. He was getting free labor for his darned old newspaper! And his farm, too. She shot him a dark glance as she recalled him mentioning that Bailey and Rudy would take care of the livestock chores. The man might be a nice guy, heart big as the whole outdoors, but what it came down to was that Joe was an exploiter! Sure, he thrived on his farm. Why shouldn't he, when he had other people doing all the work?

"Every week," Carol said happily.

Sara thought of her clean, efficient Chicago office with its quiet computers, bright lights, and sparkling chrome desks. This was the Dark Ages, and if any paper earned the name the *Wart,* it was Joe Dancy's. She crossed her arms, nodding tersely as Carol showed her the morgue—old-fashioned newspaper jargon for the clippings file—a ratty metal cabinet that appeared determined to rust from the inside out.

"You want a soda?" Carol asked. "There's a refrigerator over there."

"Over there" was a corner, dark and grimy. "No. Thanks anyway." Sara chewed her lower lip. "Are you sure your hand's okay?"

"Oh, yeah. Don't worry." Carol smiled broadly. "The doctor gave me a tetanus shot."

Sara took another portentous look around the dusty, cluttered room. She was glad Carol had received that injection.

Joe had come up beside her, and a sidelong glance at him told Sara he was barely restraining himself as he waited for her reaction. Well, he wouldn't have a long wait.

"Shouldn't we go?" she asked him, planting a smile on her face for Carol's benefit. "Nice to meet you," she told Big Ed, shaking her hand again.

"You hated it," Joe said when they got outside, kicking a crumpled paper cup halfway across the street. "I know it's a long way from Chicago, Sara." He sounded earnest as he held the truck door for her, trying to shove Staff toward the center of the seat despite his insistence on covering as much of it as he could. "And it's gone downhill since my mom died," he added, climbing in the driver's side. "But don't you think it has a certain charm?"

He gave her a pleading look, but Sara was unmoved.

"How could you?" she demanded tightly.

He looked at her blankly.

"How could you use Carol and Eddie like that? 'A little work on the paper,' you said. I assumed they were just biding their time, puttering around until they got ready to move on. But you've got them working under deplorable conditions. What about Carol's hand?"

"Hey, what's the matter?" he demanded softly, his eyes taking a concerned inventory of her expression. "It's just a cut. It's been taken care of. Come on, Sara. You're upsetting Staff."

The teasing statement was meant to soften her angry mood—Staff was lying on his back between them, snoring—but it only made her angrier. He was just too skilled at playing the good old boy, at turning the other bristly cheek when she vented her fury on him, at pretending he wanted nothing from her and Carol other than the pleasure of their company! He was even better than John at pretending her money didn't make any difference.

She glared at him. "What's the deal, Joe? Did you want me to stay in Iowa because you figured sooner or later you could sweet-talk me into working on your newspaper, too? Was that it? Your reporter quit—"

"Sara—"

"You just happened to help Carol and Eddie out of the goodness of your heart! And now, all of a sudden you just happen to be short-handed at the paper. If you think I'm going to be your next cheap laborer, Joe, you're wrong."

"Listen to me." He caught her wrists in his huge hands and brought them together against his chest, making her lean toward him and look into his face. His jaw was tight, and the humor had left his face. The sky-blue eyes that always looked into hers so frankly had hardened. "This is crazy, Sara. One hundred percent bona fide nuts. John's dead. I'm not him." She pushed at his chest, her anger coalescing into a white-hot rod that burned its way down her spine. He held her tight, but his voice was gentle now. "You're still angry with him, Sara, and you're beating your fists on the rest of the world in frustration. And that's not doing anybody a bit of good, especially not you. Honey, I'm not after your money or your reporting skills—or your gorgeous body." He gave an abashed smile. "Oh, hell, yes, I *am* after your gorgeous body, and there's no use denying that."

"Joe, please."

"Now, you just listen." When she opened her mouth to protest again, he shook his head gently and said, "Shhh. Just listen. I promise you'll feel a lot better when I'm through. All right?"

She didn't agree. But she stared at him hopelessly, knowing he would have his way, as usual. The grip on her wrists relaxed, and he twined his fingers with hers, smiling down at her.

"Yes, a reporter quit, and yes, we're short-handed. But it was Carol's idea to work on the paper. I tried to talk her out of it, but in case you haven't noticed, she has a big case of hero worship where you're concerned. She's been as proud as a little kid because she thinks she's doing something her big sister would approve of. Now, did she look unhappy to you?" He cocked his head quizzically.

Sara took a deep breath. "That doesn't mean you're not using her."

"You're a tough one, Sara," he said with rueful shake of his head. "Now listen carefully. We're going to try this again. Your sister is working hard, yes. And so is Eddie. They both feel useful for the first time in their lives. And Dad and I put them on salary two days ago."

Her head swung up sharply. "What?"

"We can't afford to pay them a lot, but between them they're getting what the reporter who quit got."

"Joe! Why the hell didn't you tell me that in the first place?"

"Because I don't like to see you reduce everything to dollars and cents. That ain't all there is, Sara," he said quietly.

"Aw, Joe." She ducked her head and squeezed his fingers, not knowing how to make it up to him. "Oh, Joe," she repeated, "I'm sorry." Her voice was weary. "I don't know why I said all that. I couldn't have really believed it. I was trying to protect Carol, but . . . I think I was protecting myself instead." She let her head fall forward and rest on his shoulder, their interlocked hands nestled against his chest. "I don't want to get hurt again. And when I stop feeling angry, I start feeling hurt." She took a shaky breath. "And I stopped feeling angry when we first made love in the camper."

"Sara." His voice was a husky whisper. "I made love to you because I wanted to, pure and simple. Lord, I could promise to take away your anger and hurt and wear us both down to shadows with how hard I'd try. But it's something you've got to do yourself. I don't think you're the kind of woman who wants a man telling her what to feel, or how deep to feel it."

She had to smile at that. "No, I don't suppose I am."

"There, you see?" He planted a soft kiss in her hair. "Just give us a chance. We handled that just fine, now, didn't we?"

"Mmmm." She could hear a fly droning in the truck, and the sun beat down on her back through the windshield, but she didn't want to move. "I really am sorry I yelled at you, Joe," she whispered.

"Oh, hell, Dad's done a lot worse." He kissed her hair again.

They sat like that for what seemed a long time, but neither moved. Staff, sprawled on his back, continued to snore.

"Joe?" she whispered against his shirt.

"Hmmm?"

"Your dog really smells bad."

He chuckled softly. "Yeah, I know. He's been out rolling in the manure again. You want to go now?"

She sighed. "No, I think I can stand this a little longer if you can."

"Yeah, I think I can stand it a little longer myself."

# Chapter Eight

SARA MADE TWO kinds of cookies that afternoon: chocolate chip and peanut butter. Joe inhaled appreciatively when he came in from the fields. He grabbed three hot cookies from the rack, juggling them from hand to hand. He munched two of them, his hip leaning against the counter while Sara dropped more dough on the cookie sheet. His eyes followed her every move. "You know what?" he said, licking the crumbs from his fingers.

"Don't tell me you just ruined your appetite for dinner," she said.

"No, but you're ruining my waistline." He smiled mischievously.

Sara eyed his waistline skeptically. As flat and muscular as ever. No flab there. "Are you sure they're not settling in your head instead?" she suggested, popping a piece of cookie dough into his mouth.

He placed his forearms on the counter and leaned forward, grin widening. Sara felt an answering tug on the corner of her mouth, "I thought you liked cookies," she said, wiping her hands.

"I do. You've found my Achilles heel. You've got to stop baking cookies every time you feel bad about hollering at me, honey. I'll gain weight."

She stared at him, hands on hips. "I holler at you a lot?" She took a deep breath, preparatory to showing him just how loud she could holler, but his look stopped her. Oh, hell, he was right. She felt so bad when she got mad at him, she never knew how to make it up to him. And so far she'd always been wrong. Joe still wore a half-smile, as though fascinated by watching her expressions change. And why *did* she get so mad at him? Why did she always think the worst? Maybe he was right. Maybe she was still yelling at John . . . "Well, you're right," she admitted. "I do holler at you a lot."

"Guess that's partly my fault?" he asked with the half-questioning inflection of someone hoping for a denial.

"Not really," she said softly.

"Well that's good."

The screen door banged, and Sara stepped back as if she and Joe had been caught embracing.

"Hey, cookies! Great!" Bailey pulled off his work gloves as he strode into the kitchen. His jeans were dusty, his shirt streaked under the arms with sweat. Joe was in pretty much the same state. They'd been running the tractor in the soybean field all afternoon. Bailey grabbed a cookie and talked around it. "Chocolate chip. My favorite. Sara, you're too good for Joe Dancy. Run away with me. I'll give you the sun and the moon." He snatched up another cookie and rained kisses on it.

"The sun and the moon, hell," Joe groused. "You'll give her a major headache and nothing else."

"I'm wounded to the quick, Joe, and I mean to the quick," Bailey protested, running a bony hand through his rust-colored hair. He affected as indignant a look as he could muster and, shaking his head sadly, left the room whistling.

Carol chattered all through dinner, and J.D. smiled indulgently as she asked him questions about the newspaper. "She's turning into quite a reporter," he said proudly, and Carol glowed with pleasure.

She helped Sara clear the dishes after dinner and began drying as Sara washed. Joe put the plates away, then yawned and said that if they'd excuse him tonight he needed to carry water to the hogs.

A peaceful silence reigned in the kitchen after the screen door closed on Joe. Out on the front porch the voices of Eddie, J.D., Bailey, and Rudy rose and fell as the lightning bugs winked on and off over the lawn. Sara stared down into the dishwater, smiling faintly as she remembered Joe urging everyone to take plenty of cookies for dessert. When she glanced up, she saw Carol watching her with an amused smile. "Not you, too," Sara said, rolling her eyes heavenward.

"Not me too what?"

"Nothing. It's just that you're the second person today who's decided to just stand in this kitchen and grin at me like a silly fool."

Carol's smile broadened. "Joe?"

"Who else?"

Carol laughed. "Look at you, Sara!" she crowed.

Confused, Sara glanced at her own dark reflection in the kitchen window. She smiled, then looked helplessly back at her sister.

"My big sister, the woman voted Most Likely to Wear a Designer Suit, is now wearing jeans, a plain cotton shirt, and loose, tousled hair. And she's elbow deep in dishwater."

Sara flushed. "I guess it slipped my mind to look in a mirror before dinner."

Carol shook her head. "But I like you this way, Sara. I've always loved you—you're my sister. You took care of me. But it's like the real you is finally coming out. And I figure Joe has had a lot to do with that. He's good for you."

"Was I such a terribly stuffy taskmaster when you lived with us?" Sara asked idly, her hands swirling in the water. She didn't look at Carol.

Her sister seemed to consider before answering. "Not stuffy. And you were always understanding. You didn't get on me about things that weren't important." Carol carefully set a glass on the counter and frowned. "But you never seemed . . . well, happy. You reminded me of someone who was sleepwalking. You weren't like that when you were in high school, at least not as I remember. I think John took the life out of you. It was as though you had to be perfect in every way to please John, the way we both had to be perfect to please Dad."

"Oh, Carol, I'm far from perfect. If you thought—"

"But you always did the right thing, Sara. I'd be off somewhere making an ass of myself, knowing you'd have to bail me out, and while I was busy screwing up my life, you were doing everything right. You didn't make mistakes, and I wanted so much to be like you."

Slowly Sara took her hands from the water and dried them. "I wouldn't change you for the world. You know that, don't you?"

"Well, *I* sure would." Carol laughed. "I always wanted to be like you. Sure of myself, knowing what I'm doing. That's why I love it here. Finally Eddie and I have found a place where we'd like to stay for a while. And I love the paper. I know it's nowhere near as grand as your job was. But at least I feel useful. I want you to be proud of me."

"Oh, Lord," Sara whispered, a catch in her voice. "Honey, I've always been proud of you. Please don't try to be like me. I'm not what you think."

"Sara, what's wrong?" Carol pulled her sister to the kitchen table and hovered over her until Sara was seated and staring at her tightly clasped hands on the smooth wood. Carol sat down beside her and chewed worriedly on her lower lip. "Is it about Joe?" she asked anxiously.

"No, honey. Your perfect sister found out a few months ago that her husband had been squandering her money—without breathing one word to her—and they would have been broke in a few years."

"You mean John—"

Sara nodded. "He knew how much trouble we were in, how much he'd lost with his poor investments, but he hid the truth from me." She decided not to mention the gambling debts.

"It wasn't your fault, Sara. No one could be expected to know about that. No one would have suspected John."

"That's just it," Sara said gently. "When you love someone you trust him. It's that 'you and me against the world' thing. And when that person betrays your trust..."

"You're afraid Joe will let you down, too."

"Did you ever feel like climbing a tree somewhere and throwing rocks at everyone who walked by?"

"All my life." Carol sighed.

"Well, that's how I feel. It's largely why I left Chicago."

"You *do* like Joe. Don't you?"

Sara thought a moment before answering. "Yes," she said softly.

"Well, I'm glad to hear it." Carol smiled. "Eddie and I have talked about staying on here permanently."

Slowly Sara nodded. She wasn't going to object. Maybe Carol and Eddie had finally found what they'd crisscrossed the country looking for. She stood up restlessly and let the dishwater out of the sink. "I'll try to get back here to see you when I return from Europe."

Carol took a plate from the drainer and began to dry it. "You know Joe would do anything for you, don't you?"

"Then maybe he ought to come to Europe with me and handle my schedule," she said lightly. "You know how disorganized I am when I travel."

"Can you picture Joe trailing in your wake, toting your suitcases and passport?" Carol giggled.

No, she couldn't. A more accurate picture came to mind—Sara in Joe's wake, running after him in her jeans and plain shirt and baseball cap, hollering at him for all she was worth...

Sleeping late was wonderful, Sara thought as she surfaced briefly to semiwakefulness, saw the clock through one bleary eye, and snuggled back down into her pillow. Joe had awakened her early on one pretext or another every day of the ten she'd been at Twin Oaks. Well, today she was determined to elude him. The previous night she had hand-lettered a crude sign and taped it to her bedroom door: *"Anyone who touches this door before noon will be drawn and quartered."*

So why was she hearing intermittent, muffled blips of rock music in her room? And were those really small male faces she'd glimpsed around her bed before her eye clamped shut again? Cautiously, she tugged the sheet up to her chin and slowly opened one eye. A cluster of little boys' faces stared back at her. Quickly Sara shut her eye again, convinced she was dreaming.

Or had she been transported into some rock video version of "Snow White and the Seven Dwarfs"? Could that have been Sneezy she glimpsed snuffing and wiping his nose on his shirtsleeve?

"Good morning, Sara," came Joe's cheerful voice.

Too damned cheerful! Sara cringed. "I know this is only a nightmare, Joe Dancy, so you might as well get

yourself and your motley crew out of my dream right
now."

She felt the bed sag as he sat down, and his voice
became cajoling. "Now, Sara honey—"

"Please," she grumbled sleepily, burying her head
deeper in the pillow and pulling one corner over her ear.
"Didn't you see the sign? I want to go back to my dream.
I was lying on a beach in the south of France, eating
Swiss chocolates..."

"They sunbathe in the buff over there, don't they?"
he asked, a note of interest creeping into his voice. *"Au
naturel?"*

Sara glared at him through a slitted eyelid. "I was
not"—she glanced at the boys—*"Au naturel,"* she muttered in a low voice.

A muffled blip of rock music broke the silence in the
room, and over his shoulder Joe said, "Murray, watch
that."

A small boy's irritated voice came back. "Cheez, Joe."

Sara dared a glance over the end of the bed and saw
a child of about nine, his black hair cut in the latest punk
style. He was readjusting the earphones of his Walkman.

"We brought you breakfast," Joe whispered.

"You're not really here," she mumbled. "You *or* your
little friends."

"Now, Sara." He affected a wounded tone. "This is
my baseball team."

"These are the Baltimore Orioles?" she said. "It's hard
to believe they won a World Series."

"These aren't the Orioles," he corrected her. "These
are the Junior Kernels."

She was beginning to feel interested, despite herself,
and rubbed a hand over her eyes. "They're all colonels?
No privates? No sergeants?"

"Very funny. Kernel as in corn." He brushed a lock
of hair from her face and grinned down at her. "Our

sponsor insisted on the name." His grin widened. "Frank's Fertilizer."

"The one with pow," they said in unison, and this time she couldn't stop herself from smiling. Control was slipping fast, as Joe's hand continued to smooth back her hair. Suddenly Sara remembered something. She gave him a suspicious frown. "So just what are you doing in here, anyway?"

"I brought you breakfast in bed," he said coaxingly. He whistled over his shoulder. "Hey, George. Front and center with the breakfast."

Sara hid another smile behind a discreet cough as George, a plump boy whose striped baseball uniform threatened to burst at the seams, hurried forward with a tray. "Thank you, George," Sara said solemnly as he set the tray on the bed and withdrew, wiping a smidgen of chocolate from his mouth. "This is very nice." She eyed the breakfast—juice, coffee, scrambled eggs, bacon, and a doughnut on which the chocolate icing was marred by a single small furrow.

"You're evading the issue, Joe," Sara said sternly, sitting up in bed and pulling the sheet up to her neck.

"And what issue is that?" He crossed his arms and favored her with a tantalizing grin.

"The sign," she repeated. "The sign on my door. You deliberately led your team in here despite a written order not to enter."

Joe shook his head. "Not quilty." He stood, a gleam of mischief sparkling in his eyes. "We didn't disturb the door. We came in through the window." She stared at him and then at the open window, the curtains billowing softly in the morning breeze. She turned back to Joe and his ear-to-ear grin. "You came through that window with a baseball team of small boys and a breakfast tray?"

"That's about the size of it."

"You're crazy, Joe Dancy, totally crazy." Her voice trailed off.

The boys were shifting their feet restlessly and giggling.

"Hey, Joe," Murray called loudly, "let's get going."

"Put a lid on it, Murray," Joe said with just enough authority to make the boy retreat into his Walkman again. "Now, Sara," he began, raising his eyebrows and taking off his cap to scratch the back of his head, "we Junior Kernels did not act without self-interest in delivering this early morning repast at great risk to our personal safety."

Sara sighed. "What do you want, Dancy?"

"We need a center fielder."

"No way. I don't have the strength at this hour to get out of bed, much less play baseball."

"Just for our practice," he pleaded. "You could stand there and hold up a glove if something happened to come your way. And I say 'happened' because these guys are not power hitters. They're good players, but we rely on strategy, Sara, not the long ball." The last was uttered with coachly pride, and Sara sighed again.

"Oh, all right, I'll be one of your Niblets, but just this once."

"We're Kernels," he said lightly. "But you can call us Niblets as long as you play center field. Enjoy your breakfast. We'll see you on the field soon as you're done." He turned toward the door and said, "Come on, boys. We're going to practice shagging flies until our center fielder finishes breakfast. Now say thank you to Sara."

"Thank you, Sara," came the dutiful chorus of voices, and there was a great deal of giggling and shuffling of feet toward the door.

Something else suddenly occurred to Sara. "Hey, Joe!" she called, and he popped his head back in the door. "You couldn't have come in the window," she said. "We're on the second floor."

He snapped his fingers. "Son of a gun. I guess we came through the door, then." He backed out, grinning, just as she threw the pillow.

She appeared on the practice field, which was actually a level stretch of pasture, after hastily gulping the coffee and the eggs. She'd put on her usual jeans, shirt, and sneakers. Joe plopped a baseball cap on her head and handed her a fielder's glove.

He had divided the boys into two teams, and Sara's team took the field. She stood between the other two outfielders, Murray with his Walkman still firmly in place—she wondered if it held his ears on—and Jeffrey, who seemed more interested in a bug crawling along the grass than in fielding. A cow observed them from the shade of a tree, mooing at regular intervals.

It was soon obvious that the boys idolized Joe. Except Murray, but Murray seemed to be on another plane of existence, anyway.

"Hey, Joe, how's this?" a player would call as he took up a batter's stance.

"Widen your feet a little," Joe would call back, stopping the game to show the boy how to adjust his posture. "Great," Joe would say after a while, signaling for resumption of play. "Now hit it out of the park, Slugger." And they did. So much for non-reliance on power hitting, she thought wryly as she chased down an embankment after the third ball hit over her head. The cow gave her a wide-eyed stare. "He'd have you running after the baseball, too, if he thought you could fetch," Sara muttered.

Finally the half-inning ended, and the first batter from Sara's team stepped up to the plate—actually it was a real dinner plate, a plastic one he assured her wasn't used for eating anymore—and drew Joe's praise by hitting a double. Then Murray took a hefty swing and lofted the ball down the third-base line. Jeffrey hit next. When it was Sara's turn, she rested the bat on her shoulder and stood ramrod straight. The first pitch sailed right past her.

"No, no, no," Joe said. He strode up, shaking his head mournfully and calling a time-out for a coaching session. "Now spread your legs farther apart—yeah, that's it—and bend your knees. Good." He went on with his advice, positioning the bat, changing her grip, and making her feel like a contortionist. All the while he kept moving her arms and legs and hips where he wanted them, with firm hands. When those same hands came to rest on her hips as Joe explained the correct swing, Sara leaned back slightly. She felt his hands tighten. "You, uh, you don't want to grip the bat too tightly." He sounded distracted, and Sara couldn't seem to loosen her death grip on the bat.

"Is this okay?" she murmured.

"Yeah, that's nice." His hands were making small circles on her hips now.

"Hey, Joe," the pitcher called. "You gonna teach her to bat or dance with her?" The catcher giggled loudly, and Joe cleared his throat brusquely, moving away from Sara.

"All right, cut the clowning," he muttered. "Cory, throw one in here. Not too hard."

Cory wound up and let the ball fly over the plate. Sara stood and watched it.

"So what was wrong with that one?" Joe demanded, standing back from her.

"It looked high."

Joe shook his head. "Too high! Suddenly she develops an eye for the strike zone. All right. Swing at this next one. I don't care if it's over your head, just swing."

The next pitch wasn't over her head—it was at her feet. And Sara swung. Joe groaned.

"All right, all right. Here. I'll help you." He stepped up behind her and wrapped his arms around hers, his hands closing over her own.

"That looks weird, Joe," Cory complained.

"Pitchers are temperamental by nature," Joe muttered

in Sara's ear. To Cory, he bellowed, "Just pitch the ball, Cory!" Sara's ear was still ringing as Cory wound up.

As Joe guided her swing, their hips swayed and brushed together, and Sara wasn't sure where her next breath was coming from, much less the pitch. She lost the use of her muscles anyway when Joe touched her like that. She let him do the swinging, and not only did they miss the ball, but at the last moment they lost their collective balance. They wobbled a moment, and then Joe sat down on the grass, pulling Sara on top of him. The bat lay on the plate, and Tony, the catcher, had doubled over in laughter. The pitcher was hooting hysterically.

Sara made no move to get up, and allowed her weight to rest against Joe. He seemed in no hurry to move either, and his fingers lightly stroked Sara's thigh. She was discovering that Joe's was no after-sunset, lights-out libido like John's. Joe's sensuality pervaded every area of his life, and he made her aware of her own. She was fast becoming a woman who thought about cool sheets and her lover's touch at noon.

"Honey," Joe whispered huskily. "Sitting here with you on my lap is going to become embarrassing in about ten seconds."

Sara hastily scrambled to her feet, and Joe got up and bent over to brush dirt from his pants, his eyes darting her a warm glance.

Sara assured Joe she had the hang of batting now. As he called the teams back into play, she stepped up to the plate. And to her immense surprise she connected with the next pitch, sending the ball sailing over the outfielders until it fell next to the cow, which let out a startled moo.

"Hey, all right!" the catcher shouted as Sara rounded second.

During the following innings, she hit four more balls, each a solid base hit. In the ninth inning, she socked a homer. The ball landed somewhere in the Venus looking glass, so they all had to stop playing and hunt for it.

"Power hitter," Joe said, shaking his head as he looked at her with new admiration.

After the practice game, George ran up, red-faced and panting. "Sara, can you play with us for the rest of the summer? Allen throws up in the car, so his mother won't bring him all the time." Allen was the absent center fielder.

"That's a very nice offer," Sara said, "but I won't be here for the whole summer, George. I'm going on a trip."

"Do you have to?" George pleaded.

"I'm afraid so," Sara said, ruffling his hair.

"Aw, gee, Sara," he grumbled, kicking a loose stone with his toe.

Smiling, Sara glanced at Joe, but something had died in his eyes, and he looked quickly away.

A car turned into the driveway. "Hey, there's my mom!" Jeffrey shouted. Three boys ran to the car with him, and they all waved as they pulled away. The next car left with two boys, and the next took several more, and Sara looked around to see only Murray left. He was sitting on the ground cross-legged, snapping his fingers in time to the music of his Walkman.

"Hey, Murray, where's your mom?" Joe demanded.

"Huh?"

"Your ride," Joe said louder.

Murray pulled up one earphone. "Mom had to get her hair done. She told me to catch a ride."

"The rides all left, Murray."

"Oh. Yeah."

"Come on," Joe said, tossing Murray's glove at him. "We'll drive you home."

Murray, for all his punk appearance, lived on a farm, and Sara marveled at that fact as they stopped the pickup truck beside a pasture gate. "Thanks," Murray called as he jumped out. He climbed the metal gate and strode jauntily across the field, his earphones firmly in place.

Joe had avoided Sara's eyes since her comment about

the trip, and now they both seemed hesitant to break the
silence that stretched between them. She watched fence
railings and undulating fields glide by as the truck bounced
down a rutted road that ran parallel to a stream. Every
once in a while she caught a flash of water bubbling over
a rocky bed beyond which cornfields gave way to open
meadow and grazing cattle.

The truck slowed as Joe took a turn, and directly ahead
of them Sara saw an old iron bridge with a plank floor.
Joe pulled the truck to the side of the road, parked halfway into a patch of tall weeds, and turned off the ignition.
"Well," he said somberly, "at least I can tell Miss Mary
I did my duty." He ran his hand through his hair. "This
is McFeeters Bridge."

"Can we get out and take a look?" Sara asked.

"If you want," Joe replied indifferently.

She gave him a brief glance and climbed out, taking
huge steps through the weeds. She stood a moment at
the approach to the bridge, looking around slowly. The
road was gravel, and well-trod paths led off into the
weeds on either side. They were a testament, she supposed, to the number of lovers who had congregated here.
She turned toward the sound of gurgling water and began
to climb down a path of dirt and stone. A lone spindly
oak struggled above the surrounding grass and weeds,
and Sara used it to keep her balance. When she glanced
over her shoulder, she saw Joe leaning against the truck,
arms crossed. He had put on a pair of sunglasses, and
she couldn't tell if he was looking at her or not.

The stream was shallow, the water clear, and the stones
and sand on the bed were grainy and several times mag-
nified. When she bent down she could see a few tiny
minnows darting into deeper water. She squatted by the
water for a long moment, thinking about Joe.

"The water's pretty cold," he said from behind her.
"Some of us kids used to wade here in the summers."
When she glanced around at him, she noticed he still

wore a remote look, though he had pushed the sunglasses up onto his head.

"While I'm here, I'd like to work on the paper, Joe," she said quietly.

That got his attention. His eyes swung to her as she stood up and faced him. He frowned, but Sara tilted her chin determinedly.

"I don't think that's such a good idea," he said.

"And why not? You're short-handed, and I've got experience. And I'd be working with Carol."

"I don't see any point in your starting something you aren't going to finish," he said bluntly, jamming his hands in his pockets. He shrugged. "About the time we got to depending on you, you'd just be leaving."

"Joe, I'm asking if I can help out on the paper. I'm not planning to take it over and sign up for your pension plan. Or medical benefits."

"We don't offer medical benefits," he said stubbornly. "We can't afford them. Hell, we can't afford to get sick."

"Then why are you turning down my help?" Her eyes blazed at him, and she held her arms rigidly at her sides.

"I already told you. Because you're not staying."

"That's the whole trouble with you, Joe Dancy," she snapped. "You'd like the whole damn world to operate on your plans. No, I'm wrong on that," she amended sarcastically. "You *expect* it. Well, I'm sorry, but I can't fall in line with your schedule. I need to get away and sort things out. I'm going to Europe."

Joe took off his cap and slapped it against his thigh irritably. "Dammit, Sara, I've never known a woman as stubborn as you."

"*I'm* stubborn!" She planted her fists on her hips.

"Yeah, you heard me. You get an idea in your head, like going to Europe or working on the *Mart,* and an earthquake couldn't shake it loose. You can sort things out just as well in Iowa as in Paris. In fact, you can sort things out a damn-sight better here where you speak the language and you're surrounded by friends."

She stared at him wearily. He was precisely the reason she couldn't sort things out right here! How could she think straight or make a rational decision when her emotions ran like a herd of rampaging horses every time he came near? He wouldn't pressure her, he'd said. Well, there were all kinds of "pressure." She didn't have to be actively sleeping with Joe Dancy to feel his effect. It was like trying to work a jigsaw puzzle while you were riding a roller coaster. Not only impossible, but likely to make you sick in the process. And that was Joe Dancy, she thought. The biggest, fastest, most spine-tingling roller-coaster ride in the world. Hell, Paris would seem tame after Iowa.

It was her trip to Europe that was bothering him; that was as plain as the scowl on his face. And she knew him well enough to understand why. Europe represented glamour, money, sophistication. Everything the women in his past had sought from a baseball superstar. They didn't want Iowa or a farmer, and by choosing Europe she was saying the same thing.

"It's not Iowa," she said quietly, trying to reason with him. "I love this place."

"Then what is it, me?"

She knew there was a lot behind his question, and he would spot a lie in a second. She didn't think she could lie to this man anyway. "Yes," she said. She watched his face fall and then his attempt to assume an expression that showed he wasn't hurt. "But not for the reasons you think," she added. "I—care a lot about you, Joe, and it's not easy for me to make the right decisions here."

"Well," he said slowly, "I guess that's a start."

A start toward what? she wondered, but she wasn't about to ask *that* question.

She stepped closer and slowly placed her hands on his chest, spreading her fingers and feeling his heartbeat lurch in response to her touch. She stared right up into his face, willing herself not to go weak-kneed and lean against him. This was important to her, and she wasn't going to resort to any seductive wiles. "I want to work on the paper, Joe," she said softly but firmly. She wasn't going to promise to stay. He would have to accept that.

He looked at her for a long time, his eyes making a slow assessment, and she felt the hidden recesses of her body come to life as though the sun had touched a cold, lonely heart with a beam of warmth. He was so beautiful, she thought distractedly, loving the formidable jut of jaw that could relax so quickly in laughter, the way his solemn eyes gleamed when he teased her, and the feel of his stubble-roughened chin against her skin as he kissed her. His hands were so big that her own felt lost in them, lost in a place where the rest of the world couldn't reach her. Safe. Her whole body experienced this when she was locked in his embrace, feeling more right than she'd ever felt in her life. More in tune with the world . . .

*Oh, God, she was in love with him!*

She sucked in her breath at the sudden realization, even as her conscious mind argued that no, it was too soon, too fast, too wrong. But inside she knew.

Joe drew her close with a soft murmur that seemed to say he couldn't help himself. His hands cradled her shoulders, thumbs caressing them in circles before he moved his fingers down her back to press her hips against his. And she responded without reserve, tilting her face up to his, eyes closing heavily. His mouth crushed hers bruisingly, and she gave the full measure of what he demanded, a passion equal to his own. There was no hesitation on her part. Her lips parted, and she stretched up on her toes to kiss him back forcefully, locking her arms around his neck, rubbing her mouth against the roughness of his mustache. Their bodies strained together with a natural rhythm that soon had them breathing raspily.

"Joe," she groaned when he finally lifted his head.

He held on to her shoulders tightly. "We'd better get back to the truck," he said hoarsely, "or I'm afraid I'll do something right here that will get us both arrested for public indecency."

He tried to smile, and it was lopsided, one of the things she loved most about him, the way he accepted his emotions and didn't bother trying to hide them. In a moment he was back to his old ways, tugging her up the bank and toward the truck, stopping before he handed her in to ruffle her hair, all in his irrepressibly high-handed way.

He started to turn the ignition key, then stopped and faced her, his expression serious. "I'm trying hard not to push you, Sara, what with John and all. I know you're feeling a little confused about everything right now. But I just want you to know that I'm having a hell of a bad time. I stand under a cold shower for an hour every night, and then I lie in bed and chew on my blanket." She smiled, and he raised his eyebrows and shrugged. "I just wanted you to know this, in case you're in the kitchen one day just minding your own business and I come in and bite you on the ear, then ravish you right there on the kitchen table."

Sara laughed. "Thanks for the warning."

Joe brushed a stray lock of hair from her forehead, his eyes caressing her in a way that made her flush. "One other thing."

"What's that?"

"If you really want to work on the paper, you can start tomorrow."

"You mean it?"

"Yeah. I'm a sucker for a woman in jeans and a base-ball cap."

"I've noticed."

He hummed tunelessly on the drive home, and Sara leaned back and closed her eyes, trying to figure out what she was going to do about falling in love with Joe Dancy. The first thought that crossed her mind was that it was pointless to worry about it. The last vestiges of her sanity would crumble in another week or so anyway.

# Chapter Nine

SARA MOVED TOWARD the door of the *Wart,* as she still—now affectionately—called the paper. Suddenly Carol bustled past, headed toward Big Ed at the Linotype, the recipe page clutched in hand. "Hey," Sara called. "I've got to go to a church supper! Where's the camera?"

Carol had a pencil clenched between her teeth; she nodded toward the counter. When she had handed the paper to Big Ed, she removed the pencil. "Over there, on the counter. I used it this morning to get a shot of the county Pork Queen. Don't keep it out too long. Mrs. Erhardt wants it back early tonight."

Sara sighed as she took the camera from the counter. "Makes me feel like I'm taking a widow's only son on his first date." She had discovered during her first day's employment on the paper that the Polaroid, inadequate as it was for a newspaper, didn't even belong to them. It was on loan from Mrs. Erhardt, two streets over. "By the way," Sara said, turning at the door as she juggled camera, purse, and notebook, "the Linotype is ours, isn't it? And the printing press?"

"Far as I know," Carol said, grinning. "But I think Big Ed's on loan."

"Ain't on loan!" Big Ed called over the racket of the Linotype. "Just biding my time till the right fella comes along." She nodded emphatically and pulled the hem of her Madonna T-shirt.

Sara went out the door, humming to herself. She took J.D.'s car, an ancient VW, because he insisted that people working on the paper not use their own cars. "We pay you paupers' wages as is," he said cheerfully. And he was right, Sara acknowledged en route to the church, gears grinding as she shifted. Not that she minded. She felt less an appendage and more a part of the little paper's lifeblood than she'd ever felt at her job in Chicago. For some reason, everything seemed more real here. Even the sky looked like something you could touch if you wanted. Chicago was rapidly becoming a fading memory, and John's deceptions no longer made her heart ache.

In the church basement, Sara fumbled with the Polaroid while two elderly women pressed fried chicken into her hands. She finally got everything in order—the two chicken thighs wrapped in a napkin and stowed in her purse, and the flash in place on the camera. The women posed happily before an enormous deep fryer, thanking Sara profusely for the publicity. A young woman rushed up, wringing her terry-cloth apron in her hands and wailing that she had just dropped Mrs. Lorenzo's famous devil's food cake on the floor. "Now, don't you worry," the older woman said. Her name was Mildred, Sara had learned. "You just go down to the bakery and pick up a devil's food cake there. I think that's Mrs. Lorenzo's secret recipe anyway. That woman can't boil an egg." Then when the woman ran off to do her bidding, Mildred turned worried eyes on Sara. "Oh, dear, you aren't going to mention the cake in your article, are you? We advertise homemade desserts. Mrs. Lorenzo would be terribly upset—and I wouldn't want anyone to think we're cheating with bakery cake!"

"Of course not," Sara soothed. "Your secret's safe with me."

She left a relieved Mildred in her wake, thinking about what her former editor, cynical Mark Thompson, would have made of that story: CAKE SCANDAL—CULT PEDDLES FAKE DESSERT. Sara smiled. Iowans had their own set of values, and she doubted Mark Thompson would understand. They didn't seem to care that Good Samaritans had gone out of fashion in some parts of the country. Joe had spent most of this week on a neighboring farm, hauling hogs to market because the farmer's truck had broken down, then working on the truck himself. He'd come home late each night, and Sara had watched through the bedroom curtains as he got out of his pickup, stretching and rubbing his neck wearily. There were moments when she regretted that he wasn't pressuring her . . .

But she pushed that thought aside, along with other thoughts of Joe, and pulled her reporter's notebook from her purse. Then she went inside the plain brick county office building and took a seat in the back row of nine folding chairs. A few farmers and their wives sat in front of her as the county supervisors, dressed in either bib overalls or old suits—no sophisticated sportswear here, she'd discovered—talked among themselves. She took shorthand notes when the meeting got under way, but she soon abandoned that and just listened, fascinated.

A resolution was duly presented by one of the supervisors to designate July 29 as Edgar Durks Day in the township. Edgar Durks, it was explained, was the man who had overturned his hog truck on the highway the day Sara and Joe went shopping. While Sara was wondering why this should earn him a day named in his honor, one of the commissioners explained that a certain loose hog—one Prissy Belle—had stopped to wallow in the mud in a large pothole in the middle of the state road that ran parallel to the highway. A vacationer snapped a picture of the hog, and the picture made the front page of another newspaper in the state. An issue of that paper in turn made its way to the governor's office. The end result was that the governor had promised to sign a bill allocating funds for repair of the state road. The farmers in the area were all ecstatic, because they used the road every day. A farmer in the front row raised his hand and, with incisive common sense, suggested that a day might more rightly be named for Prissy Belle. But the supervisors voted this down, preferring to lay the credit at Edgar Durks's door. Edgar stood up and took a bow, his apple cheeks shiny and pink with excitement.

The back door opened, and everyone turned around at the sound of squealing. In came a florid woman in bib overalls—Mrs. Durks, Sara surmised—driving a pig in front of her. The pig ran straight to Edgar and began snuffling at his shoes. "Prissy Belle!" Edgar called, obviously delighted. "And Amanda."

Sara snapped a photograph of Edgar and Amanda posing proudly with Prissy Belle, the board members clustered in a beaming circle around them. Then Edgar eagerly told the board, and anyone else who would listen, tales of how smart Prissy Belle was. As she left the room, Sara smiled to herself. After all, she had just witnessed the birth of a legend . . .

Carol was rooting through the tiny refrigerator when Sara got back to the office and wearily set the camera on the counter. A bird-faced woman in a feathered hat jumped up from a chair. "I thought you'd never get back," she said anxiously.

"This is Mrs. Erhardt," Carol called, her voice echoing in the caverns of the refrigerator. "She needs her camera."

"My daughter's visiting with the new baby," Mrs. Erhardt explained, "and Eldon just had his first solid food. I want to take a picture."

"Will you bring the camera back?" Sara called out after the woman, more than a little worried as she watched her dart out the door with the prize.

"She took it last week, too. She needed pictures of her price-winning petunias," Carol explained. "Got any gum?" She opened Sara's purse and pulled out the chicken thighs in their greasy napkin.

"Ooooh. Do you mind?" Without waiting for an answer, she bit into the chicken, and Sara observed privately that Carol wouldn't care if the chicken had been in Sara's purse for a month. She had once watched her unpredictable sister eat chocolate that she had dropped on a sidewalk where pigeons were known to congregate.

Wearily, Sara sat at her desk and rested her head in her hands, thinking about the odd entity that was the *Wart*. And then she began typing copy for Big Ed to set: her stories on the church supper and the official recognition of a local hero.

"Looks like you had a fun evening," Big Ed commented as the Linotype clatter filled the room.

Slowly Sara began to smile. "Yeah, you know, I really did." Actually there was something very endearing about the *Wart*. She leaned back and laced her fingers behind her head. She closed her eyes and hummed tunelessly, her voice blending with the racket of the Linotype.

She heard the door close and glanced up to see J.D. coming in. He looked tired.

"For a minute I thought Joe was here," he said, and when she looked puzzled he said, "The humming," and grinned.

She stopped, realizing for the first time that she had

taken up one of Joe's habits. Or maybe she had caught it the way you catch poison ivy. By close contact.

"I need to talk to you, J.D.," she said seriously, slowly sitting up and placing her hands on the desk.

"This sounds ominous." But he was smiling indulgently, the way he smiled at Carol. It was the kind of look that made Sara feel she belonged here, with his son.

He sat down on the edge of her desk, and Sara said, "You've been out selling ads since early this morning, haven't you?"

"Now you really sound like Joe." He laughed. "Are you going to lecture me, too, Sara?"

Sara shook her head. "J.D., I hate to just walk in here and then start making unwanted suggestions, but we really need a camera. Something that takes print-quality pictures and that Mrs. Erhardt won't come in and snatch when her grandbaby comes to visit."

"I take it she repossessed the Polaroid again."

She nodded. "And the headliner spit out two blank headlines today. And Eddie said the press is being held together with baling wire." She cleared her throat, wondering how far she could go. "And these typewriters, J.D." She shook her head as she surveyed the antique on her desk, feeling that words were inadequate. Today something had come loose in the carriage bar, and she now had to roll it by hand after each line.

J.D. said nothing for a moment, raking his hand through his hair in that same way Joe did. "I know, Sara," he said in his kind voice. "It's got to be tough for you working here. Can't seem much like Chicago. Joe didn't want you to work here at first, and I think that was why. He loves the paper, and he didn't want you to criticize it. Well, I can't blame you if you want to call it quits."

"Oh, no, J.D. I really like the paper. It grows on you," she added quickly.

He was silent a moment. "I wish I could buy a new printing press and new typesetting equipment, even a new camera." He smiled, a light kindling in his eyes. "Joe's mom and I—we used to wish for things all the time. You lie in bed at night, and one of you starts it—'I wish I had that'—and then the other says, 'Yeah, and I wish I had this.' Pretty soon we'd get going so fast we'd start laughing. Sometimes Joe and I get going on that our-selves over coffee in the morning or at dinner when some bill comes due." He gave her a gentle smile. "Do you ever make wishes, Sara?"

"Lots of times." *I wish Mother and Dad would stay home for Christmas instead of going to Bermuda*. That at nine. *I wish John would say one thing to me that I could be sure wasn't a lie*. That at twenty-nine. And now? *I wish Joe would*...She frowned, not sure what it was she wished Joe would do. "It always boils down to money, doesn't it?" she said sadly.

"You don't strike me as the kind who lets money bother you a heck of a lot."

Sara shrugged. "I'm not so sure I know myself at all anymore."

"Why do you say that?" said the older man shrewdly. "Does it have anything to do with Joe?"

"Sort of."

J.D. nodded and looked down, studying the desk. "He has a stubborn streak, like his mother, but you can count on him, Sara. Just remember that. One thing Joe knows, and that's what's important and what's not."

Sara was silent.

J.D. looked at her, his brow furrowing. "You're not going to cry, are you?"

Sara laughed, her voice strained. "Not at the moment anyway."

"Well, that's good to hear, because I'll tell you some-thing Joe and I haven't told many people. Sara, we can't afford all those things the paper needs, not even a decent camera at this point. Joe put all the money he'd saved into the farm. I've been feeding my savings into the paper, but it looks like it won't be enough."

"You mean you might have to sell the *Weekly Mart?*" Sara met his frank gaze, disturbed by the possibility of J.D. losing his wife's legacy.

"I hope it won't come to that," he said, his voice level. "If Joe has anything to do with it, the paper will stay in our family. My son is fiercely loyal, and he considers selling the paper tantamount to selling his mother's memory. Well, he wouldn't be far from wrong." J.D. got up from the desk and stretched wearily. "I know Joe," he said with a grim smile, "and he'll do anything he can to keep the paper."

"J.D.," Sara said hesitantly, "I've got money if you need it."

He scratched his chin uncomfortably. "That's nice of you to offer, Sara, but I don't think Joe would go for that."

"And what does Joe have to do with my donating money?" she said stubbornly.

J.D. raised his eyebrows. "Everything. This paper is his as much as mine." He cleared his throat. "Sara, I know I'm treading on delicate ground in a pair of clod-hoppers at the moment, but I guess I know how Joe feels about you. And if I was hard put to guess, I'd say you've got some feelings for him. And that's a kind of sticky situation between a man and a woman. And a gift of money could cause a considerable problem."

Sara stared down at the desk. "J.D.," she said, shaking her head sadly, "if I live to be a hundred I'll never understand men."

When she looked up, he was grinning. "My wife used to say that. Claimed men were downright ornery."

"I'm sure she was a very smart woman," Sara said.

"She was," J.D. said. He headed for the stairs. "Got to check the press. See you later." She heard him chuckle just before he disappeared down the stairs.

Everything always came back to Joe! Sara was negotiating an emotional maze, and she kept running into blind alleys. She knew that when she finally rounded the right corner and got to the center of the maze, there would be Joe. There was just no escaping it.

J.D. seemed sure of Joe's feelings, but Sara wasn't. She felt she was engaging in a game of blindman's buff. "Loves me, loves me not," she muttered whimsically, her typewriter keys substituting for daisy petals. More to the point, her subconscious warned, you should be playing He wants something, he wants it not.

After all, he had Carol and Eddie working on the *Wart*, and despite his initial objections, Sara had now joined the staff. Had he planned it that way all along? Of course not! she railed at herself. Joe simply wasn't that devious.

But some persistent devil from Chicago reminded her of J.D.'s words: Joe would do *anything* to keep the paper going . . .

The trouble was, she just couldn't think straight anymore. It was as if some tornado right out of *The Wizard of Oz* had picked her up by the heels in Chicago and dropped her on her head smack in the middle of Iowa and Joe Dancy's life. And her head was still spinning. In fact, she wasn't at all sure who she was anymore.

Once she had considered herself the embodiment of an independent woman—self-assured, competent, not tough but at least invulnerable to messy emotions. But that was in Chicago. Here in Iowa some other woman had emerged—coaxed from the shadows by Joe. And this woman was a stranger to Sara. She was vulnerable, lighthearted, and fast becoming addicted to the gentle teasing and warm laughter doled out by one Joe Dancy. She was a woman who cared deeply what happened to all of these wonderfully human people she'd just met; a woman who wanted to share some of the earthly pleasures they had found in this remote corner of Iowa. At the same time the old Sara, the woman who had been cheated of love and money by her husband, kept delivering dire warnings about illusions, Joe Dancy being a prime example. And Sara kept looking over her shoulder as if afraid that some new heartache was sneaking up on her.

Evening stole over the town, and streetlights winked on as Sara helped Carol finish pasting up the front page. Downstairs the rumbling of the printing press was punctuated by a string of oaths from Jenkins. Sara's back was stiff, and she straightened to massage it as the door opened. She stifled a yawn before she turned and saw Joe. He looked so tired. And there was more than a vestige of strain around his eyes. Her first impulse was to go to him and put her arms around him, but she made herself stand still.

"I got done over at the Henderson farm and I wondered if you were through here," he said.

"We just finished." Sara nodded toward the newly pasted front page.

"Would you like a ride home?" With his cap in his hand like that, he might have been begging a favor of a duchess, and Sara's heart went out to him.

"Sure."

Carol picked up the paste-up board and started for the stairs. "I'll tell J.D. you got a ride." She stopped at the stairs and looked back at them, and when Sara met her eyes she read frank concern. Suddenly her baby sister was the protective one. *Oh, God,* Sara thought. *Everybody in the world knows what's going on between Joe and me.*

She walked to the truck with Joe, aware of his soap-scented skin and damp hair. He had apparently hurriedly showered before coming to her, and already her flesh was tingling in anticipation of his touch. When his hand trailed down her spine as he helped her into the truck she felt her knees wobble in excitement.

The palest tinge of rosy daylight hung in the west like

a silk scarf. Blinking on and off in the darkness were the first stars, faint and hesitant, peeping from the scarf like silver sequins.

"Rudy, Bailey, and Miss Mary are at home playing gin rummy and drinking beer," he said. "I think they're smoking cigars, too, Lord preserve us."

She smiled in the darkness of the truck. She loved to hear him talk, his voice as smooth as velvet. He was like the evening breeze rising over the fields, making the cornstalks toss in the starlight. "Who's winning?"

"Miss Mary at last count. Rudy may have to marry her to pay off his debt." He gave her a quick glance, too strained to be casual, and looked back out the windshield. "Would you mind if we stopped at the camper?" he asked hesitantly.

"No, that would be fine." Her heart was pounding.

The truck window was down, and she rested her head against the seat, letting the cool air blow her hair. He turned down a dirt path that ran between two fields, the hulking silhouette of trees in the distance. When he stopped the truck she realized they were behind the camper, well out of sight of the house. She got out and followed him silently into the camper where he lit a kerosene lantern and set it on the counter, adjusting its wick. He patted the bed, and they sat down side by side. Sara stretched her legs out in front of her and slid back against the wall, but Joe leaned forward and stared at the floor, tense despite his obvious weariness.

"This week has been a granddaddy of a bruiser," he said. "All I could think about was how much I'd like to come home and wrap my arms around you. But you were in bed before I hit the driveway. And, of course, I'd promised not to pressure you."

"I hear you come in every night," she admitted. "I don't fall asleep until I hear you go past my door on your way to bed."

He reached out and took her hand in his, threading

his fingers through hers. "How are things at the paper?"

"All right," she said evasively. "Tell me about your week."

"You don't want to know."

"If I'm correct, I'm sitting here in the dark in your camper, because you've got things on your mind, and you don't want to go home to a houseful of people," she insisted stubbornly. "So tell me about your week."

She could see the flash of his smile through the dimly lit interior. "Damn, you're a saucy woman, Sara." He squeezed her hand when he said it. Then he leaned back against the wall, his shoulder touching hers. "Things were getting to me this week. Sometimes I feel like I'm trying to hoist a grand piano to a second story window with a ball of twine. Something's going to give, and the whole thing's going to come crashing down."

She thought immediately of the paper. "It can't be easy for you, trying to manage the farm alone," she said carefully.

"The farm's only half of it. Bailey seemed determined to be a real bastard this week. I've been running around half the county in my spare time, scouting up job prospects for him, and he says, 'Hell, Joe, don't go to any trouble on my account. I'm not down to bare-bones broke yet.' I came close to punching him out last night." He sighed, and she felt his fingers move restlessly on hers. "And then there's the paper."

He fell silent, and when he didn't continue, Sara said, "I asked J.D. about replacing some of the older equipment at the paper, and he said there wasn't any money."

She saw Joe close his eyes. "Yeah, that's about the size of it. The economy's tight now. We're having some trouble getting advertisers. Hell, Dad's out on the street twenty hours of every twenty-four trying to sell space, but it's not going to work. I talked to the bank today about a loan."

"A loan?" she asked in alarm.

He nodded. "I offered the farm as collateral."

"Oh, Joe."

His hand tightened on h s. "Whatever happens, I will not let the farm or the ▮▮er go," he said with such determination that she knew it would take a bulldozer to raze the idea from his mind.

She stared off into the darkness, frowning. Her thoughts shifted in a dizzying kaleidoscope—John, her trust fund, Iowa, Joe, the newspaper, John...

"You don't have to take out a loan," she said hesitantly. "I can give you the money." There, she'd said it, and caution be damned. It was time she stopped looking back over her shoulder at the past, and threw herself into the present. She tried not to think of the doubts in the back of her mind—J.D. had said Joe wouldn't take her money. But what if he was wrong? And what if Joe did take the money—and stopped wanting her?

"No, Sara. I wouldn't take a cent from you. Thank you, but no."

"But, Joe—"

"I don't want your money, Sara, and that's that."

The implacability in his voice was unmistakable, and though he didn't change position, his spine stiffened perceptibly. Despite J.D.'s warning, she hadn't expected Joe to be so stubborn and so foolish. Sara felt a growing sense of outrage. She was offering him a way out, for goodness' sake! Didn't he understand?

She pulled her hand from his. "Don't you see? You don't have to go to a bank for a loan. I can give you whatever you need. You'll have the farm and the paper and no worries."

"No worries?" he demanded. "Is that how you see it? A little money will solve everything. Is that the sum total of *us*, Sara?"

"Don't make it sound so cold and mercenary," she snapped. "I'm not buying you, for goodness' sake."

"Aren't you? Haven't you been trying to add me up

in dollars and cents ever since you got here? How much does he want from me? Is he after all my money or only part of it? Tell me that's not true, Sara, because I'd like to hear you deny it."

"Maybe at first," she admitted, her voice tight. "But things have changed. I want you to take the money."

"Salve for your guilt, Sara? You'll give me the money, and that will repay the debt you feel you owe me? Then you can skip off to Europe with a clear conscience."

"I'll skip off to Europe, as you put it, at least knowing you won't lose what you value the most."

He gave a hollow laugh. "I'm in danger of doing that if I take your money," he said in a low voice. "Don't you see? It would always be between us, like some barricade."

"No, I don't see," she snapped. "What's between us is your stupid pride."

"Maybe you're right," he said with an odd note of detachment in his voice. "But my pride's not for sale."

"For pity's sake!" she exploded. "You'd let your farm and newspaper, the two things you care about most, go down the drain for want of money that's been offered to you? That's not just pride! That's stupidity."

"Thank you for clarifying that," he said sarcastically. He stood and moved to the door. "I'm too tired to argue with you tonight." He blew out the lantern, and Sara voiced murderous thoughts beneath her breath as she groped her way to the door after him. He waited just long enough for her to negotiate the step. Then he slammed the door and stalked off toward the truck.

"Will you kindly take small steps?" she finally called in exasperation. "A person could get a heart attack trying to keep up with you."

She realized it was too late anyway—they had reached the truck. He opened the door for her, his eyes narrowed angrily. He climbed in his own side, and they drove back to the house in silence. He didn't wait this time, either, and Sara sat scowling in the truck as he strode toward the house. "Hey, Dancy!" she hollered out the window after him. He stopped but didn't turn around. "Remember how you said life moves at a different pace around here? Well, you were right. It's at least three times faster than where I come from." She climbed down and walked with dignity to the front door, despite the fact he'd already gone inside, banging the screen.

# Chapter Ten

IT WAS EARLY Saturday evening, and Sara had been released from her duties at the *Wart* until Monday. She was celebrating by sitting in the old tire swing that hung from an ancient and massive cherry tree outside the back door. Dinner had ended an hour ago, and she and Carol had finished the dishes. Eddie and Bailey were feeding livestock, and Rudy was repairing a fence by the cornfield. Joe had taken the truck into town on an errand.

Joe hadn't met her eyes since the previous night in the camper. J.D. and Carol had tiptoed around the two of them as if walking through a mine field. Only Bailey had remained unimpressed with Joe's irritable manner. When Bailey had commented on Joe's new after shave at dinner, Joe snapped, "Can it, Bailey. I'm in no mood."

"Yeah, well maybe that's your whole problem," Bailey shot back. "Any fool man who can act that way around Sara ain't worth his salt anyway." And with that he stomped out of the house.

"Oh, for crying out loud," Joe had groused after his friend's departure.

Now Sara spun slowly in the swing, watching a lightning bug blink on the ground. She heard a truck slow down and glanced up to see Joe turning into the drive. Stubbornly she stayed where she was, rocking from side to side. The truck stopped in the drive. Joe hopped out, carrying a paper bag. He stopped a moment when he spotted her on the swing, then squaring his shoulders, walked deliberately toward her.

"I'm back," he announced as he stopped before her.

"I was breathless in anticipation," she replied.

"Oh, yeah?"

"Yeah, I could hardly digest dinner for all the excitement."

Joe stared at the ground a minute, poking at it with his shoe. "For some reason I didn't think you'd be glad to see me."

"And why is that?"

"Damned if I know. Must be some female quirk."

"Hmph."

He cleared his throat and held up the bag. "Dad always told me that women like flowers and candy. The problem is, I didn't know what kind you like."

Sara stared at the bag. "What kind did you get?"

Joe opened the bag and looked in. "Well, I have daisies and roses and carnations and chrysanthemums and baby's breath. And an orange tree."

"You've got all that in there?" she said skeptically.

"Sure." He set the bag down at his feet and began filling his large hands with bunches of flowers. When he finished he had a fat bouquet in his right hand and a miniature potted orange tree in his left hand. He looked at her hopefully.

"Any violets?" she asked.

He shook his head.

She looked at the flowers and pretended to consider. "I think I like the daisies best. Although roses are nice, too. And baby's breath."

"Here, take them all." He piled the bunches of flowers in her lap and set the orange tree at her feet. "Now, the candy. What do you like?"

She glanced at the bag and said, "Maybe you ought to just read me the list."

At that he began to pull candy bars from his pockets. "Well, we've got Snickers and Hershey bars and Peppermint Patties and Butterfingers and Three Musketeers."

She couldn't help it. His gravity undid her, and she started to smile. He grinned back happily and began to pile candy bars on her lap, on top of the flowers. "Did I do okay?" he demanded.

Sara laughed. "Yes, you did great, Joe. But if I ever go shopping for a new car I'm not taking you."

"Can I have one of your candy bars?" he asked.

"I thought these were a present!"

"Well, I didn't eat much dinner. I'm just a bit hungry, and I thought you'd want to reward me for my thoughtfulness."

She sighed. "All right. What do you want?"

"The three Musketeers. And maybe a bite of the Snickers."

She handed him the appropriate candy bars and then deeply inhaled the mingled fragrance of the flowers. "You really know how to give a girl a present."

In the growing dark she could see the white of Bailey's T-shirt as he and Eddie walked toward the house from the hog pens to the accompaniment of clanging feeder pans. Staff came loping across the soybean field and ran for Bailey.

"Jeez, Joe!" Bailey cried. "That dumb damn dog of yours tangled with another skunk."

Bailey and Eddie began running toward the house, Staff trotting behind them, oblivious to Bailey's string of epithets and Eddie's continuous spitting, as though trying to rid his mouth of the smell. As they drew close, the odor of skunk became more pronounced.

Joe shook his head. "That dog has the brains of a walnut. He thinks skunks are cute, and about once every month or so he tries to romance one of them."

Sara gathered her flowers and candy and started for the back door.

"Hey, where are you going?" Joe called.

"You think I'm staying around for this?"

"Aw, Sara, come on. After all, I'm the man who brought flowers and candy."

"And I appreciate them very much, I'm also going to remove them from the vicinity of the skunk smell." With that she pulled open the screen door.

"You're coming back to help, aren't you?" Joe called after her hopefully.

She watched from the kitchen as Bailey and Eddie gained the back yard, dashing past Joe in a mad race for the door. "What a dumb dog!" Bailey hollered over his shoulder. "Really the pits, Joe," Eddie added. Staff trailed in their wake, merrily wagging his tail.

Joe stood under the cherry tree, shaking his head, his thumbs hooked in his belt as everyone disappeared into the house. He looked down at Staff and rumbled, "Jeez, dog, you stink." Methodically he set about dragging a huge washtub from the garage, and Sara watched as he filled it with water from the hose. He shook his head as he looked down at Staff and made a face, apparently at the stench. He picked up the paper bag from under the cherry tree and fooled with it for a moment, then plopped it over his head. Sara grinned when he turned around and she saw the holes he had punched for eyes. Now the bag was a makeshift gas mask. She couldn't let him give Staff a bath out there all by himself. Well, she just couldn't.

He was just too cute, and he probably was banking on that.

Before she tentatively opened the screen door a few minutes later she took one of the pinch clothespins from the hanging bag in the closet and put it on her nose. In her hands she carried a plastic bottle of bubble bath she'd brought from Chicago.

She couldn't see Joe's expression through the paper bag. "He smells terrible," she muttered through the clothespin as she poured bubble bath into the tub. The paper bag nodded in agreement.

Joe lifted Staff into the water, which was now pink and swirling with bubbles, and they began to soap him. The only sound for several minutes was the splash of water, loud gasps for breath—hers and Joe's—and intermittent howls—Staff's. Sara felt like howling along with him. "He does stink," she groaned.

The bag nodded.

As they scrubbed the dog and then rinsed him off, Sara couldn't resist teasing Joe. "Does Staff do any other tricks, Joe? Besides fetching skunks. Like showing burglars where the key is?"

The bag was observing her.

"Do cats chase him up trees?"

"Now, Sara," a muffled voice inside the bag began.

Sara giggled, then jumped to her feet and out of the way just as Joe lunged for her. She backed up, laughing. "Now, I was just trying to boost Staff's spirits," she said as Joe pulled off the paper bag. A devilish gleam lit his eyes. He advanced on her in earnest, and she flicked a stray soap bubble at him. Staff leaped from the tub, filling the air with pink bubbles, and Sara ran after him, laughing. Joe caught her around the waist from behind and pulled her to the ground. Pinning her down, he began to nibble ravenously on her neck, his body crosswise over hers. Her legs kicked in the air, and she gave in to a fit of laughter as he made growling sounds deep in his throat.

He began to plant rapid, moist kisses on her face, finally landing one on the tip of her nose, just below the clothespin. "I do love a woman with a wooden nose!" he whooped, ravishing her neck again, sending her into new gales of laughter.

Her hand curved around his neck, and in the next instant his mouth became seductive and teasing. Sara sobered. She was kissing him back in earnest when they both heard the screen door open. Without looking up, Joe said, "Go back in the house, Bailey. I'm not going to listen to anything you tell me."

Bailey cleared his throat. "It's the phone, Joe." Something in his voice made both of them look up. "You'd better answer it." Bailey cleared his throat again.

Sara trailed after Joe to the kitchen, lingering at the door and leaning against the counter while he picked up the phone on the opposite wall.

She fiddled with the bowl of fruit on the counter, rearranging the apples and grapes, hesitant to stay and listen, but unwilling to leave.

Bailey had gone through the house to the front porch, and through the front screen Sara could see him sitting with Eddie and Carol. Nobody was talking, and only an occasional creak of their chairs broke the silence.

"Yes, Mr. Hawkins, thank you for calling," Joe was saying. "Yes, you're right. I did want to know as quickly as possible." Absently Sara twisted the stem of an apple. "Yes, I understand," Joe said after a long silence during which Sara could just barely hear the murmur of a deep voice on the other end. "Sure, I know." Joe sounded so tired! "Yes, well, I appreciate your taking your time to call on a Saturday. Yes... Thank you... All right... good-bye." Joe hung up the phone and stood for a long moment, staring at the wall.

"Joe?" Sara said softly.

"It was the bank," he said without turning around.

"The loan?"

He shook his head. "Farms are losing money, newspapers are losing money. The whole damn world's losing money, so banks aren't loaning any. Even banks are losing money," he added wryly. His big hands were spread on the counter, and Sara stared at them, her eyes tracing the strong, capable fingers, nicked and toughened by farm work. Her heart kicked into the familiar triphammer beat, and she swallowed, remembering the feel of those rough hands, so gentle on her flesh.

The apple stem snapped off suddenly in Sara's hand, and she stared at it, so lost in thoughts of Joe that she didn't remember how the apple came to be in her hand. She set it down and walked to Joe, placing one hand on top of his. He turned and pulled her against his chest, resting his chin on her hair. "It's all right, Sara," he murmured, comforting her. "I can make it without the loan."

"Joe—" Her voice was trembling, and she had to stop.

She felt him gently shake his head. "No, honey. Shhh. Don't let's talk about money now."

They stood that way for a long time, listening to the sounds of night settling around them, the crickets, frogs, and a whippoorwill outside and the quiet hum of the refrigerator in the kitchen. Only when a chair creaked on the front porch did they stir. A pair of headlights was coming up the driveway, and Joe said, "That's Dad. I'd better go talk to him." He held Sara away from him carefully and looked down into her face, his blue eyes sad but undefeated. "Don't worry about it, honey. Everything's going to be fine."

She watched him go out the back door, straightening his shoulders, and she loved him more than ever. He seemed the very embodiment of the farm—strength, endurance, quiet dignity. He and J.D. were solid, dependable men who loved with all their hearts. And how did Joe feel about her? Did she hold a claim on his heart? Or was she just the Chicago woman who was going to leave for Europe? Sara shook off the thought and watched

Joe greet his dad. Deep in talk, the two men ambled away from the garage, and Sara turned away restlessly. She didn't feel like facing everyone on the front porch, so she slipped out the back door and went around the side of the house to the hill where she and Joe had stood looking over the meadow with its Venus looking glass. She could hear the cattle lowing and the rustle of grass as they bedded down for the night. She sat down on the damp grass and hugged her knees to her chest. She listened to the sounds of the night and watched the lightning bugs blink on and off, and she felt a measure of comfort.

"Wake up, Sara," a male voice called cheerily, and she'd had enough practice at identifying that voice in the wee hours of the morning to know it was Joe.

"Well, if it isn't the human alarm clock," she grumbled into her pillow.

He chuckled. "Come on and get up, honey. We're going to the Old Threshers Reunion today."

She poked a hand out from the sheet and held up one finger. "Number one, I'm not old." Up came a second finger. "Number two, my name is Scott, not Thresher." Up came a third finger. "And number three, I'm not going to a family reunion of old Threshers."

He laughed and pulled the sheet from her face. "The Old Threshers Reunion is a fair. There are demonstrations of old-time threshing equipment, and a carnival."

"Mmmm." He was stroking her hair, and it felt so good.

"And food stands, Sara. Homemade fudge and funnel cakes."

She yawned broadly. "Well, it does sound kind of interesting."

"I knew I could convince you," he said triumphantly. "Just appeal to your stomach."

"That sounds terribly close to an insult," she muttered, opening her eyes around another yawn and fixing her sleepy gaze on him. A quick and treacherous thought entered her mind—it would be nice to wake up beside him every morning. The warmth began spreading up from her toes, and her blood played reveille in her veins. He had apparently just gotten up. He was wearing a red plaid robe, and his hair and mustache were in disarray, giving him a dangerously attractive air, like a cowboy roused from his sleep beside a campfire. Even in the faint morning light, she could see the amusement in his blue eyes. "I can't believe it," she muttered.

"What's that?"

"There is actually the beginning of light in the sky. As though the sun were about to come up for something. How come you didn't wake me while it was still pitch dark? As usual?"

"An oversight I'll have to correct," Joe said.

"Well, don't bother on my account," Sara retorted.

Grinning at her, he swatted her rump and left the room, humming his usual tuneless song. "The man drives me crazy," she mumbled as she staggered out of bed and groped her way into her robe. "Correction. He has already driven me crazy." She began pulling clothes from a drawer. "I've totally taken leave of my senses. Why else would I be getting up before dawn just to talk to myself?"

Sara braced herself as she entered the kitchen. Those Dancy Special sandwiches for breakfast again—she knew it! He was spooning scrambled eggs onto slices of bread, and he smiled over his shoulder at her as she entered. Sara walked pointedly around the sandwiches as if they might reach out and cling to her neck, and rummaged in the cabinet for a box of doughnuts. At the kitchen table Bailey, Rudy, J.D., Carol, and Eddie were drinking coffee, eating those sandwiches—yech!—and talking about the trip. Joe and J.D. must have told everyone about the loan being turned down, because when Sara came in the night before, there had been a gloomy pall hanging over everyone on the porch, and talk had been subdued. But the loan wasn't mentioned, and Sara could imagine Joe reassuring everyone that things would work out. That was the problem with Joe—he felt he had to be responsible for things working out for everyone he ran into. He would have made a terrific Santa Claus, and she wouldn't be surprised if he didn't try to fulfill that fantasy at some children's party every Christmas.

"Here's your sandwich, honey," Joe said on the way to the truck. He handed her one of the foul concoctions. "Got to have your protein, you know."

Giving him a baleful stare, Sara sighed as she climbed into the truck between Joe and Carol. With his eyes on her, she dutifully consumed it.

As was her habit, she fell asleep on Joe's shoulder during the drive. When she woke up, the truck was bouncing over a rutted road, and the crew in the back— Bailey, Rudy, Eddie, and J.D.—kept hollering at Joe to take it easy before they "busted their buns," as Bailey put it.

Just ahead was a mammoth fairgrounds. It was mid-morning already, and the rhythmic strains of calliope music reached them. The midway was just awakening, a Ferris wheel beginning to revolve slowly, its empty cars swinging, a Tilt-a-Whirl stretching its octopus arms in a circle. Joe parked the truck in a field, in a long line of other vehicles, and they all got out and stretched.

"You're going to love this, honey," Joe promised, looping his arm around Sara's shoulders.

As they walked toward the fairgrounds, more sounds greeted them, the bleats and grunts and bellows of sheep, pigs, and cattle, the hiss and rumble of machinery, the chunk-chunk sound of tractors and the sizzle of food frying in Lord knows how much cholesterol. The sights and odors were equally mingled. Down one path were the livestock barns on the left side, the brightly painted food carts on the right. The odor of manure met the aroma of hot dogs and French fries somewhere in the middle of the path. Beside the midway lay the fields where threshing demonstrations were to take place. Something was happening in one field, and Joe tugged Sara in that direction.

"I got to get me some coffee," Bailey muttered, taking off in the other direction.

The group split up, with Joe hollering that they were to meet back at the truck in four hours.

Sara stepped over bundles of cable running from the midway and picked her way over straw and grass paths, Joe's arm still around her. They joined the crowd at a split-rail fence and rested their right feet on the bottom rail. There they watched as six teams, each composed of one man and two heavy draft horses, walked around in a large circle, all pushing at what looked like the spokes of a wheel. The spokes were mounted on a circular device. A man standing in the middle of the circle explained that the machine was actually threshing oats. After a while, Joe took Sara's hand and moved her on down a row of old tractors. He readjusted his red cap and grinned at her. "Ever tasted a funnel cake?" he asked. When she shook her head, he said, "You have led one deprived existence, lady," and trotted her toward the nearest stand.

She ate the funnel cake, licking powdered sugar from her fingers, and had to admit she had indeed been missing something. Joe's next stop was in a long line waiting to enter a livestock barn. "Bluegrass concert," Joe explained. The line moved slowly past a dairy shed where cows occupied open stalls, their tails busily brushing at flies. Each cow had a sign over her head, and Sara began reading these as she passed. "Blossom," said the first sign. Under the name was other vital information that Sara took to be Blossom's age and milk production. Under "dam," it said, "Daisy May" and "Flower Girl." There were two names under sire as well—"Matthew" and under that, "Joey Baby." It was the same with Amy,

Ethel, Edna, and Clovis. Sara poked Joe. "Look at that," she said, pointing to Miriam's stall. "How come they have two names under both dam and sire?"

"Hmmm?" Joe glanced at the stalls idly, then said, "Oh, that. There was a divorce in the family."

Sara stood in place, frowning, as people inched up behind her, gently nudging her forward. By the time she realized she'd been had, Joe was hiding his smile by rubbing his mustache. He rocked on his heels, humming out of tune. When she punched his arm, he jumped. "Ow!"

"Serves you right," she muttered, "making fun of a city girl."

His grin appeared quickly. "I couldn't help it. You were so cute, asking me about cows." He ruffled her hair. "Some dairymen list both dam and granddam, and the same with sire. There. How's that for a crash course in dairy cows?" When she didn't appear mollified, he said, "You know, my mom was from a city herself— Atlanta. Dad met her when he went there one summer to visit his cousin. He says he used to tease her something fierce about being a city girl. Once she asked him where Keokuk got its name, and he told her it was from the Keokuk bird that flew over the field and made a strange cry—*Kee-Oh-Kuk*." That grin was firmly back in place, and Sara vowed not to ask him how the city really got its name. She was learning that the Dancy men could not be relied upon to give a straight answer.

The bluegrass concert was loud. The three sparrows that lived inside the barn flew back and forth over the audience and chirped anxiously. There was a lot of straw underfoot, and one roll of flypaper hung from a rafter. There was only one window, and a little girl pressed her nose to it from the outside, trying to see in. At the height of the fiddling and banjo picking, Sara turned to Joe. "Is this the culture you promised me when I showed up on your doorstep?" she said, her voice straining to be heard over the music.

"Oh, hell, honey, this is only the half of it," he said, grinning. "Wait'll you see the university's cow pie sculptures."

Well, he was pulling her leg again, but when they walked outside, he drew her into his arms and promised her that one day he would take her to hear the Des Moines Symphony at their beautiful Civic Center, show her the University of Iowa whose Writers' Workshop had been attended by Flannery O'Connor and John Irving, and take her to the Amana Colonies, which were founded as a Socialist society and later produced Amana appliances. When he finished, she was dizzy with the thought of the wealth to be found in Iowa. Joe tugged her around the midway and insisted she sample the caramel apples, the snow cones, and the cotton candy. "I'm going to burst," she complained when he suggested just one more funnel cake. He finally talked her into sharing a Polish sausage with onions and green peppers. She was moaning and holding her stomach as he marched her across the midway. "You've got to ride the Scrambler," he insisted.

She hung back in horror, but he pulled her toward the gate, saying, "You don't get sick on these, do you?"

"I don't know. I never rode one before."

Joe grinned. "Well, then, it's about time you did. Come on."

The Scrambler was well named. Its main objective seemed to be to scramble the brains and stomachs of those who were foolish enough to allow themselves to be strapped into a small car and then spun in circles at the end of a steel arm. "Oh, Lord," Sara groaned. Joe was whooping and, she gathered, having a good time. "I'm dying," she gasped, unable to think of anything but what she'd eaten—the Dancy Special, the funnel cakes, Polish sausage, cotton candy, and a caramel apple. They were combining into a lethal time bomb, and she wasn't sure what would kill her first, her head or her stomach.

"What's wrong, honey?" Joe asked in her ear. "You look a little green."

"A little green!" she cried. "I'm dying here!"

"Now, honey, it's okay. The ride's stopping. See, we're slowing down. Sara?"

The instant the torturous machinery stopped and the attendant unsnapped her seat bar, Sara stumbled out of the car, groaning and clutching her stomach.

"What is it, honey?" Joe was demanding solicitously at her side. "What hurts?"

"Oh, Lord." She was batting away his hands, which kept hovering around her. "Go away," she groaned.

"Can I get you something, Sara?" He was obviously worried, but she really didn't care at the moment. "What do you want?"

"A swift death," she muttered.

"Hey, look what I found!" It was Bailey, and Sara groaned again. His timing was perfect.

Joe didn't want to talk to him, either. "Go away, Bailey."

"But look," Bailey insisted. With childlike pride he held up a piece of unfinished pine board with "Carol & Eddie" burned into the grain. "A guy over at that booth was doing these, and I had to get one for Carol and Eddie. I mean, if they're going to build a house on that five acres you sold them, they need something special to mark the occasion. Great idea, huh? They can hang this over the front door."

Sara had straightened up, still clutching her stomach, surprise momentarily blocking out sickness.

Joe was frowning at Bailey, and if looks could kill, Bailey would have dissolved into the straw at his feet. Bailey looked from one to the other, comprehension slowly dawning. "You mean you haven't told her yet?" he demanded.

"Bailey, if you don't beat all," Joe said. "No I haven't told her."

Bailey glanced at Sara worriedly. Still clutching her stomach, she groaned again. "Oh, damn, she's taking it bad, isn't she?" Bailey blurted out.

"Sara, are you all right?" Carol appeared at her side, Eddie in tow.

Sara was beginning to feel like a hospital patient with a horde of young interns clustered around her sickbed. She turned accusing eyes on Joe. "He fed me Polish sausage and cotton candy and caramel apples, not to mention his special sandwich."

"And I took her on the Scrambler," Joe confessed miserably. He tried to brush back her hair, but she pushed his hand away again.

"And I spilled the beans about you buying the land," Bailey added in equal misery, shifting his weight and running a hand through his red hair.

"This is all my fault," Carol wailed. "I should have told her about the land. I really meant to."

Exasperation overcame Sara, and she temporarily forgot about her upset stomach and spinning head. "For heaven's sake, stop talking about me like I'm not here." She rounded on Joe, who was trying to put a protective arm around her shoulder. "You," she said through clenched teeth, shrugging away from his touch, "had better have a good explanation. What do you mean, selling them land behind my back? Doesn't it ever occur to you to tell me *anything?*"

"Now, Sara, it's not what you think," he began before Bailey interrupted him with, "It's a rock-bottom price, Sara. They're getting a great deal."

Joe turned on Bailey. "Will you get out of here! Trying to explain anything with you around is harder than shoeing a horse on roller skates."

Bailey looked wounded, and Eddie intervened. "Come on, Bailey. Let's look at those old tractors over there and let them fight this out themselves."

They went off, Bailey casting worried looks over his shoulder.

"I want to know what you're up to now, Joe Dancy," Sara demanded. "You didn't breathe a word about selling land to Carol. What kind of scheme are you hatching now?"

"It's not Joe's fault," Carol said. "I talked him into it. And I'm the one who should've told you."

She glanced at Joe, who lingered for a minute, then took the hint and said, "Why don't I go find some aspirin and something for Sara's stomach?" He disappeared around the corner with a last frowning look over his shoulder.

"Eddie and I are going to settle down here," Carol said, facing Sara. "We asked Joe to sell us five acres of his land because his farm is so pretty. He didn't want to at first, but J.D. was on our side. He told Joe it would be a good idea."

"I know you like it here," Sara said plaintively, "and I understand. But why couldn't you have talked it over with me?"

Carol stared down at the ground and wiped her hands on her jeans. "I don't know," she said at last. "I guess I was afraid of what you might say."

"Why on earth would you think I'd say anything?"

"Because I've done such a bang-up job of screwing up till now. Because I wanted this, and deep down I was afraid somehow I'd botch it and you'd come running in to rescue me again. Because I wanted to do the right thing."

Sara smiled wanly. "Are you happy here?"

Carol looked up at Sara and nodded.

"Then you're doing the right thing."

"There was one other reason," Carol said, trying hard to meet her sister's eyes.

"And what's that?"

"Eddie and I like Joe and his dad a lot, Sara. And we want to live here in Iowa. But we . . . that is, I . . . well, we don't want to look so eager that we . . . mess things up between you and Joe."

Sara laughed. "Honey, if that's all that's worrying you, then put it out of your pretty head. If anyone's going to mess things up, it'll be either Joe or I. And we're pretty damned capable of doing a top-notch job of it. All on our own."

Joe rounded the corner again at that moment, glancing anxiously at Sara as if to gauge her mood. He seemed reassured and handed her a plastic cup of fizzing liquid and two aspirins. "This will make you feel better," he told her.

"I'll go find Eddie," Carol said, backing away and smiling tentatively at Sara and Joe.

"So how are you doing?" Joe asked, concern etched in his face, his blue eyes clouded. His hand reached for her, then stopped halfway as he apparently remembered her recent aversion to his touch.

"Much better," she said, trying to scowl at him. She took his hand and laced her fingers through his. "But if I catch you hiding something from me again, I'm going to whomp you a good one."

His grin appeared like sudden sunshine. "What do you want to do now?" he asked.

"I want you to go to that booth over there—see it by the hot dog stand?—and knock down three milk bottles with a baseball. I want one of those teddy bears! Then my bear and I will take a nice tame ride on the merry-go-round."

"The bear's as good as yours," he assured her happily, ruffling her hair.

Seven quarters later he bundled Sara and seven purple toy parrots aboard the merry-go-round, abjectly apologizing for failing to win the teddy bear. "My throwing arm went bad on me," he said ruefully. "Haven't been practicing enough on Dunbar."

But his arm felt just fine when it went around her waist as he straddled the wooden pony beside her, his long legs reaching to the floor. As far as she was concerned, there wasn't much of anything wrong with any part of Joe Dancy.

# Chapter Eleven

MISS MARY HAD brought some cabbage from her garden, and they had asked her to stay for dinner. Joe was on edge. Bailey had left that morning for a job interview Joe set up for him, planning to drop Rudy off at his apartment on the way. Bailey had assured Joe he would be back in time for dinner, but he hadn't shown up. Joe kept glancing at the clock, hardly touching his ham and potato salad.

"You seen Jonesie and Sam this summer?" Miss Mary abruptly asked J.D.

"Sure did. Ron the Runner was with them, too. They stopped in here a little while back."

"My husband was always fond of hoboes," Miss Mary told Sara. "A lot of 'em came through here during the Depression, and he always said those men were this

**153**

country's Gypsies. Takes an odd sort to do that in this day and age."

"Say," J.D. said, struck with an idea, "the National Hobo Convention is in Britt in a couple of weeks. Why don't we all ride up there for it?"

"Hey, that sounds great," Carol chimed in.

"You'll have a great time, Sara," J.D. assured her.

Sara cleared her throat. "Well, the truth of the matter is that I've got to get back home next week. I'm leaving for Europe in a few days."

There was a moment of silence, and J.D. murmured something about how sorry he'd be to see her go.

"Excuse me," Joe said sharply, scraping back his chair. "I think I'll go feed the hogs."

When he was out the door, J.D. shook his head. "Bailey's going to get a right smart poke in the jaw if he shows up here with some lame-brained story tonight." He shook his head again.

When Sara went to bed that night, Joe was still outside. She tossed and turned, unable to fall asleep. But she must have *just* dozed off, because she dreamed she heard a phone ring. When she woke up she could hear Joe talking softly downstairs. She put on her caramel-colored robe and tiptoed to the staircase, brushing back her hair with one hand. She could see Joe crossing back and forth in front of the kitchen light as he paced with the phone. He was still wearing jeans and a short-sleeved blue sweat shirt. She crept downstairs and stood in the shadows outside the kitchen, listening. She wanted to go to Joe, but she didn't know what his reaction would be after the way he'd acted at dinner.

"Well, that's just dandy, because I don't want to listen to your excuses," Joe was saying. A long silence. "You think that matters a hang with me? You're damn right I'm mad. If you were standing here I'd give you a sock in the jaw that would land you halfway across the room." His voice was weary when he spoke again. "Don't go

and bawl on me, because it's not going to get you anywhere this time." Joe sighed, and when he passed in
front of the light again, she caught a glimpse of him
running his hand roughly over his mustache. "Yeah . . .
yeah, I hear you . . . Sure, but I'm not telling any lies for
you—you got that? Okay . . . yeah, all right." He hung
up the phone and took a step out of the kitchen, nearly
colliding with her. His eyes narrowed. "What are you
doing down here?"

"I heard the phone. Was that Bailey?"

"Yeah, the damn fool."

"He let you down again?" When he didn't answer,
just stared at her stubbornly, she said, "I don't suppose
you'd care to talk about it, on the off chance it might
make you feel better."

"No!"

"Well, I'm glad I rank so high on your list of confi-
dantes," she muttered, her own temper flaring.

"Tonight you don't even make the top ten," he said
tersely. He snapped out the kitchen light and passed her
on his way to the stairs.

Stubborn and angry and hurting in her own way for
him, Sara followed him slowly, feeling her way in the
darkness. At the top of the stairs she saw soft light coming
from his room. Resolutely she made her way down the
hall toward it. Passing J.D.'s room, she heard the older
man snoring. There was no sound from Carol and Eddie's
room, but they were heavy sleepers and no doubt hadn't
heard anything.

Sara stepped inside Joe's room and closed the door
quietly. He turned from the desk where he'd been leaning
on his hands. His eyes blazed, but whether it was with
anger or desire she didn't know. Her own gaze dropped
to his hands, so big and rough where the golden light of
a table lamp fell on them. There was a fresh scrape on
one knuckle of his right hand. He'd probably banged it
filling the hog feeders. She'd come to know his routine

and the cadence of his life. It had come to be her own cadence.

Her courage was beginning to ebb. "Well, say something," she whispered.

"I don't know what you want me to say, Sara."

"Couldn't you at least tell me about Bailey?"

He shrugged resignedly, and she saw that the flame of his temper was spent; only dry ashes of it were left in his eyes. She moved over and sat on the bed, and he leaned against the desk, watching her with what she could only describe as wariness. "I thought it would be different with him this time," he said, looking at the tiny window over her head and not at her. "It was a good job. A meat-packing company near Burlington. He would have worked in the office." His voice was as much mournful as angry. "He let Rudy off, then turned tail and ran. He got as far as a bar in Mount Pleasant. Then he called."

She waited, her hands knotted in her lap, then said, "You can't make him live his life right, Joe. I learned that with Carol."

"Damned if I can't try," he muttered.

"Why torture yourself?" she said. "You keep throwing opportunities at Bailey, and he keeps ducking them."

"But he might take one of them," he said, "and that would make it worth all the trouble."

She remembered then how Joe had shown her the milkweed plants in his soybean field. He'd told her he didn't disturb them, because he'd read that monarch butterflies laid their eggs in milkweed. She knew Joe would always keep trying with Bailey, because that's the way he was. People mattered to him.

"Maybe you're right," she murmured. "Maybe he'll come around again. Maybe this next time it will work for him."

"It's about time something worked," he said quietly, his eyes briefly meeting hers. They were haunted and hurt, and she wanted to hold him so badly she had to force herself not to move. She had an inkling that his hurt wasn't all because of Bailey, but she wasn't sure.

"I thought things were good between us," she began hesitantly. "You know, the candy and flowers and the trip to the Old Threshers Reunion."

"So did I."

"So what happened? Downstairs you treated me like a corn borer who'd asked for the menu from your north forty."

"Don't you know?" He pushed away from the desk and moved restlessly toward her. He raked a hand through his hair, which refused to be tamed. "No, I suppose you wouldn't. I have to spell it out every time." When she still stared at him in helpless incomprehension, he shook his head slowly. He raised his hand in a useless gesture. "What does it matter anyway? You probably don't really want to know. It isn't as if you cared about—" He broke off, staring down at the floor, a pained frown creasing his brow.

"Cared about what?" she demanded, and when he raised his face to hers again, his eyes were a deep blue and filled with hopelessness. She had to ask it. "Cared about the farm, Joe? About Iowa?" She gathered her courage. "About you?"

He didn't flinch, but she nearly did. He gazed at her steadily. She stood up and walked to him, opening her robe as she went. "Hold me," she said fiercely, "and then tell me what I don't care about."

He stared at her a long moment, his eyes burning with undisguised desire, and when he spoke, his voice was hoarse. "If I touch you, Sara, I want you to care more than you've cared for anything in your life. That's what I want from you."

"Try me," she whispered.

He took her hands, his own swallowing them, and pulled her to him. He lowered his head to nuzzle her hair, breathing deeply and shakily. He was pushing open her robe, slipping his hands beneath the straps of her cream-colored nightgown to rub her shoulders. His thumbs glided over her collarbones and found the pulsepoint at the base of her throat.

She shrugged out of her robe, letting it fall to the floor, and started to take off her nightgown, but Joe caught her hands. He slid the straps over her shoulders and arms, then placed her hands around his waist. His touch gentle as gossamer, he slid the gown to her waist. Her eyes half closed in the intoxication of desire, her fingertips grazed his shirt, feeling the corded muscles bunch and move beneath her touch.

His eyes darkened as they moved over her with a lover's appreciation. "You are so beautiful," he whispered. And she did feel beautiful! In his eyes she became a flower blooming in the desert, for his eyes and touch only. His fingers caressed her breasts, circling the nipples and returning to glide silkily over them. She groaned, her knees threatening to buckle, and her hands tightened on his waist, then roved restlessly under his shirt and up his back, needing to feel his flesh.

With one swift move he stripped the gown to her ankles, kneeling before her, his mouth pressing hot, moist kisses on her belly. He stood up slowly, tracing an upward path over her torso with his tongue.

It was her turn now, and she made rapid work of it. She tugged the sweat shirt over his head, tousling his hair even more. All the while his hands were playing havoc with her senses, returning to her rib cage and stomach, teasing her with light caresses.

"You're making things hard here," she accused him playfully as her fingers fumbled with his pants.

"That's not rightly so." He looked at her seductively from beneath half-closed eyelids. "I'd say you're the one making things hard."

Laughing, she tugged down his pants. Joe pulled her close and kissed her deeply.

She had never felt this sense of urgency or of promise with John, she thought fleetingly as Joe lowered her to the bed and kicked off the remaining traces of his clothes. He was magnificent. She couldn't look at him, all raw-boned and hewn muscle, and not catch her breath. Her heart hammered as he knelt beside the bed, raising her hand to his lips. He kissed each finger and then her palm, and a maelstrom of heat swirled through her veins. With one swift movement he turned out the lamp, so that only moonlight illuminated the room.

And then he began at her ankles, working magic with his mouth and fingers as he moved slowly up her legs. She writhed as his mouth ministered to her thighs, the rough skin of his unshaven jaw rubbing the sensitive inner flesh, spurring her to even greater reaches of pleasure.

He levered himself onto the bed and knelt above her, his mouth seeking her breasts. When he straightened, Sara ran her hand down through the mat of hair on his chest, letting her palms press gentle circles over his nipples. He groaned her name and moved to her neck, nibbling and sucking and teasing her to distraction. She pulled his head up to hers, his mouth meeting her own in a hunger that seemed to grow more fierce each second.

In one swift movement he rolled over, pulling her on top of him. He was ready for her, but she prolonged the play, pleasuring him with her mouth and fingers the way he had touched and aroused her, taking deep satisfaction in the soft groans he made and the urgency in his voice when he called her name. Her blood was thick and drugged with wanting him when he pulled her up and entered her. The sweetness of their joining was even greater than the time before. This time he had demanded a commitment, and that was a torch to her abandon. She met each thrust, arching her back and pushing her breasts against his hands as he gently squeezed them. He took her nipples between thumb and forefinger and tugged and stroked until her breath came in uneven gasps.

The exquisite sensations mounted second by second as his thrusts became more powerful, bringing them both to the brink. Like the wind and the cornstalks, they moved together in a rhythm of the heart. And at the last moment they both became the wind, soaring freely into the sky, their breath and heat spent. Sara collapsed on his chest, her sweat-sheened skin against his, and her hair flowing around them. Joe gathered her in his arms, rubbing his chin on the top of her head and murmuring indistinct words that spoke to her heart.

The moonlight touched only part of his face; she couldn't see his eyes in the dark. She was lying beside him now, her damp skin drying and cooling her in the summer air. She thought he was asleep from the even rise and fall of his chest where her hand toyed with the matted hair.

"I could get the camper all fixed up by September," he said softly, his fingers tangling in her hair. "We could follow the Mississippi north toward Minnesota. The trees are beautiful in the fall. We could stop wherever and whenever we want. I'd have to be back for the combining. If it's wet I couldn't get the beans out until late October anyway, maybe November." He exhaled slowly and shifted, but she still couldn't see his face. "I guess I'm talking a lot because I'm worried about what you're thinking right now." His hand stroked her hair. "Sara?"

"I expect I'll be in Europe this fall, Joe," she said miserably.

He sat up so that moonlight splashed across his face, turning his eyes into pools of night sky. "You told me you cared," he said roughly. "Is this what you meant? You care as long as you're in my bed, and then it's bye-bye, Joe, I'm off to Europe?"

"That's not fair," she protested.

"Isn't it?" He held up her silk and cashmere robe. "I can't offer you silk or Paris. I can't compete with your money."

There were things in life that a woman needed, there were things she wanted, and there were things that didn't make a whole hell of a lot of difference one way or the other. Silk and Paris fell into the last category. "How dare you!" she hissed. "How could you even insinuate that I put you in the same category with those things? I told you you mean more to me than anything else in the world, and I damn well meant it!"

"Then don't go to Europe. Stay here with me." His voice was roughened and deep and coaxing. Oh, she wanted to hear that note in his voice, the one that begged her to stay. "I'll make you happy, Sara," he promised softly.

"But you won't take my money?" she whispered. "Even for the *Mart?*"

He raked his hand through his hair. "I want you, not the damn money."

Sara sighed and shook her head. "Don't you see that it's part of me, Joe? John couldn't come to terms with it, and now you can't."

"And what about Europe?"

"I want to go because I can't live with myself anymore. I've got to be alone, Joe, so I can find out who I am."

"You can do that here."

"Like hell I can," she grumbled, and reluctantly he smiled. "Okay," he whispered. "You go meditate on some French beach and eat Swiss chocolates. Then you think you could find your way back to Iowa?"

"No sweat. I've been dropping bread crumbs since I arrived."

His laughter rumbled in his chest. "I love sassy Chicago women," he murmured, bending to plant kisses along her throat. Sara gave a low moan and turned in his arms.

# Chapter Twelve

It was what Joe called the Big Game. He had bustled into her room before she was awake—not that that was anything unusual—and sat on the bed, announcing it was time to get up.

Sara gave her usual answer. "Go away."

"But tonight's the Big Game," he announced, appearing affronted that she didn't recognize the importance of the occasion.

"I don't care," she said to her pillow.

"I brought you coffee and a doughnut," he promised, waving both in front of her nose.

She considered, her eyes still clamped shut, the pillow wrapped around her head. "What kind of doughnut?" she asked.

"Your second most favorite. The kind with white icing." She heard him set the cup and plate on the night table.

"With chocolate sprinkles?"

"Yes, with chocolate sprinkles. I went out early this morning just to get you that doughnut."

She opened one eye. "Did you get any of those cherry turnovers?"

"You mean the ones with that thick filling and just a tiny bit of glaze on top and that flaky, buttery pastry?" he asked innocently.

"Yes!" she said.

"Let's see, now." He pretended to ponder the question as she sat up in bed. He rubbed his chin and then nodded solemnly. "Seems to me I did pick up a couple. But darned if I didn't leave them in the kitchen. Guess you'll have to get up if you want one, Sara," he said happily.

She pursed her lips and eyed him sleepily. "You do know, don't you, that I'd planned to sleep in this morning? The supervisors' meeting last night was a real bear. The sheriff was there, and he had a loose thread hanging down from the hem of his trousers. He tried to burn it off with his lighter and ended up setting the whole cuff on fire. It took three board members and the secretary to beat out the sparks. Fortunately it just singed the hair on his leg."

"What a trouper," he said, kissing her nose and ruffling her hair. "I bet you turned out a dandy story."

"I giggled the whole time I was writing it, Big Ed giggled the whole time she was setting it, and Jansen giggled the whole time he was printing it. I heard him in his dungeon." She leaned over on her elbow and sniffed at the coffee. "This smells good. You know, despite the fact that you continue to wake me up at the crack of dawn against my will, you're improving."

"Great!" he said, whacking her behind. "I'll see you in the kitchen." He left the room accompanied by his usual tuneless humming.

* * *

Now it was evening, and the Junior Kernels stood in a straight row along the third-base line. Opposite them stood a row of Jets, the rival team. Tonight was the championship game. A youthful drum and bugle corps stood behind home plate, pumping out a shaky version of "The Star-Spangled Banner." Everyone stood, the boys on the field and the men in the bleachers with their caps in hand, the women in gingham dresses or jeans, all with their hands over their hearts. Joe was standing with his boys, his coach's uniform a little short in the legs, so that the hem topped his socks by half an inch, exposing tan skin. The breeze ruffled his thick, fair hair, and it caught a glint from the field lights. He had trimmed his mustache that morning, and with his blue eyes squinting against the glare of lights, he looked as if he should be leading a cavalry charge in the Old West, not a bunch of little boys in a baseball game. He was a very handsome man, Sara thought, and she was truly in love with him. In a way she had never loved anyone in her life . . .

"Play ball!" the umpire bawled, and boys scrambled to their positions.

When the Jets scored two runs in the first inning and then the Kernels went down in order, Sara's heart sank. She knew the boys wanted to win this championship for Joe. Tony had confided in her that the boys had taken a solemn oath to do their best for Joe, because he had bought them new uniforms with his own money and they wanted to thank him the best way they could.

Things picked up for the Kernels in the fourth. Murray, minus his Walkman—he actually had ears, Sara marveled—made a diving catch, ending the inning and saving two runs the Jets would probably have scored had he dropped the ball.

The Kernels tied the game in the sixth inning. They would have taken the lead, but the third batter, George, was thrown out at the plate. Joe argued furiously with the umpire, and a chunky older woman with steel gray hair ran to the wire fence behind home plate and shook her pudgy fist at the beleaguered official. In light of her extreme involvement, Sara assumed the woman was George's grandmother. This was confirmed when the woman stopped by the concession stand on her way to her seat and came back loaded with two hot dogs, a large soda, and a Twinkie. She indeed must be a relative of George's!

The Kernels played beautifully in the seventh and eighth, and the game was still tied when the Jets came to bat in the ninth. After two quick outs, one of the Jets hit a long drive to center field. Allen, the center fielder with a propensity for throwing up—the boy Sara had subbed for in their practice game—raced toward the fence, his short legs pumping. All eyes were riveted on him. At the last moment he jumped in the air and came down with the ball in his glove. He stared at his glove a full four seconds as if he couldn't believe what he'd just done. The fans went wild, and Allen trotted in with a wide grin.

Sara kept her fingers crossed in the bottom of the ninth as the Kernels came to bat. She watched Joe, who was walking back and forth behind the bench, obviously swelling with pride. He had a word for each boy, and it was clear they adored him. The final glory belonged to George, who came to the plate with two out and nobody on. Joe had patted him on the back, and Sara heard him shout, "Knock their socks off, George!"

And George did! He connected on the second pitch and the ball sailed for the fence. Plump little George stood at the plate, mouth open, watching it go. "A home run," screamed George's grandmother, standing up so fast that her soda and Twinkie flew almost as far as George's homer. "Way to go, George!" she screamed, and the fans screamed with her, Sara included. They all came spilling out of the stands as George rounded the bases, and the Kernels gave him high fives all around. Then they surrounded Joe, their voices high-pitched squeals of excitement.

Eyes glowing with shared pride, Sara lined them up. With the *Wart's* Polaroid she captured a perfect candid of the league president presenting the team with a two-foot trophy.

"Back to the farm for hamburgers!" Joe called out, and there was a general stampede to the parking lot. J.D. was at home starting the barbecue fires, and Carol and Eddie ran past Joe and Sara, calling their congratulations.

"I've got to finish frosting the victory cake," Carol shouted.

Joe looped an arm around Sara's shoulders, and she leaned against him as they walked toward his truck. Dust rose in little clouds as cars pulled away. George's grandmother was buying him a last ice cream as the concession stand closed.

"Joe," Sara began as he pulled the truck out of the parking lot. For a moment she just enjoyed the feel of the breeze on her face and the sweet, sticky smell rising from the creek bottom. For the moment she was perfectly happy.

"What is it, honey?" he asked after a bit. Sara only smiled over at him. "What?" he repeated, grinning when her smile widened.

"I love you." She was laughing now.

"Well, I'm glad you find that so funny, sweetheart, because I love you, too."

"What a team you have!" she said, laughing. "What a coach!"

One long arm reached over and tugged her to him, and Sara sighed happily.

Once out of the truck, Joe was surrounded by Kernels and their parents, leading him to one of the picnic tables where the trophy resided in a place of honor. J.D. clapped his son on the back as Joe took over the spatula at the grill. Sara busied herself carrying things from the kitchen, then collapsed into the tire swing. Just a few feet from Joe, she was hidden in the night shadows of the cherry tree, and happy in the privacy of the moment, she watched the glow of the coals reflect on his handsome, well-loved face. He had a smile for every kid and every parent who stopped to talk to him, and even one for George's grandmother, who wondered if the hamburgers were done yet.

J.D. was stringing red, green, and yellow party lights from the trees, and Sara got up to help him. "There," he said, flashing her a broad grin as they finished. "I'll go plug them in."

Sara picked out Miss Mary sitting in the shadows at a picnic table, and stopped by to chat. "Can I get you something to drink, Miss Mary?"

"No, thank you, honey. Just sit down a minute. Now, tell me if that boy took you to McFeeters Bridge yet."

Sara laughed. "Yes, as a matter of fact."

"Well, good for him. Joseph's not as backward as I thought."

"No, he's not," Sara said, hiding a grin.

"Now, don't humor an old woman. I see that sly smile of yours. So he's been working pretty fast, has he? Well, that's all the better. He's a good man, Sara."

"I know," Sara said warmly.

Miss Mary spit on the ground and gestured around the yard. "Look at all these people. I bet there's not a one here that Joe hasn't done something for at one time or another. And that trophy is something those kids will remember all their lives. Joe's committed to this place and these people, and when that man makes a commitment, it's for life. Nothing halfway about him."

"No," Sara murmured. "Not Joe." But things did seem to be halfway with Sara. She was half a Chicago woman in suits and heels, her hair confined at her neck. And she was half Joe's Iowa lover, a laughing woman who wore jeans and didn't care if the wind mussed her hair.

Now if she could just figure out which half was the real Sara.

The party lights came on with a burst of color, and there were oohs and aahs from around the yard. "Now if that isn't pretty," Miss Mary said admiringly. "On that note, I think I'll head home. Seems like the older I get the earlier I go to bed. Must be turning into a chicken in my old age." She chuckled, and Sara helped her to her feet.

"Good night, Miss Mary," she said as the old woman made her way to her grandson, who promptly dug out his keys and walked her toward his car. Sara went back to the tire swing, lost in thought.

Joe was talking to a stout, balding man with a potbelly who was taking it upon himself to teach Joe the finer points of coaching, and Joe gave Sara a grin as she walked past.

She didn't know the potbellied man had moved away until she heard Carol approach. Sara was hanging on to the rope of the swing, her head flung back to look at the stars, when Carol's voice proclaimed, "My lawyer drew up the loan papers, Joe. They should be ready for us to sign first thing tomorrow."

Sara straightened. At that moment Joe caught her eye, seeing her for the first time. He looked suddenly uncomfortable. Apparently, though, Carol hadn't seen Sara in the shadows. "I talked to the bank and everything's okay," she continued. Her voice trailed off and, warned by the look on Joe's face, she glanced back toward the swing. Sara stood slowly and walked toward them.

"Oh, Lord," Carol said in a small voice.

"What's this all about?" Sara said, looking from one to the other. "What papers? Why is Carol involved in the bank loan, Joe?"

Carol spoke first. "It's just that you've been so touchy about money since you've been here, Sara. And then you told me about John . . . I wanted to help out. When

I heard the bank turned down Joe's loan."

Joe said it then, straight out, but it took a minute for it to sink in. "I'm borrowing the money from Carol. We're signing loan papers tomorrow. With what she and Eddie are paying for the land plus the loan, I can keep the paper going."

Joe looked more tired at that moment than she'd ever seen him. Tired and worn down. His face was already shadowed with new beard. All she could think of was *Why is he doing this to me?*

"I told you I'd give you the money," she said, the first swell of anger flooding her veins. Her heart was hammering in her throat.

"And I told you I didn't want it between us," he answered calmly.

"So you went to my sister instead!" she said incredulously.

"Sara, it was my idea," Carol interrupted.

"I don't care whose idea it was," Sara said, near tears. "I'm the person you're supposed to love, Joe. Remember me? If you wanted the money, you should have taken it from me."

"And wondered the rest of my life if you were comparing me to John?" he said. "Can you honestly tell me you would have trusted me completely with your money, after what happened before?"

"I trust you, Joe, and you know it," she cried. "It's your stupid pride. You couldn't stand the thought that the woman you love should be the one to bail you out. Good old self-reliant Joe. He can lend a helping hand to every needy soul who crosses his path, but he can't take any help from the woman he says he'll devote his life to. With me it wouldn't have been a loan—it would have been a gift—but you couldn't take that kind of help."

He looked as if she'd struck him. And for once he had nothing to say.

Sara was still fighting back the tears. "I don't know

why I stayed here in the first place. I don't belong in Iowa. All those farms and little newspapers, and baseball teams. And towns with names like Ottumwa and Keosauqua! What the hell does Keokuk mean anyway?"

With that, the tears welled over, and she began walking rapidly toward the house. She heard Carol call her, but Joe said, "Let her go. I think she wants to be alone right now."

And alone she was. She lay on the bed, staring at the ceiling, listening to the laughter and partying outside, and calling herself a fool to have thought she and Joe could make it work. She should have known he couldn't accept what she was. She couldn't escape her money.

# Chapter Thirteen

IT WAS STILL dark when she carried her suitcase out to her car and threw it in the trunk. Her hand was on the door handle when he spoke from behind her.

"Where are you going?"

She turned slowly, reluctant to look at him. The sentry light by the garage cast a bluish sheen on his skin. He wore only pajama bottoms, and his hair was rumpled. He must have been sleeping; his eyes were heavy-lidded. He brushed a hand across his mustache, his eyes roving over her tense form.

She flushed under his hard scrutiny. She had pinned her hair back at the neck. She wore a white linen suit with a red silk blouse. She had put on matching red heels.

"I'm going home," she said.

"It's three A.M."

"It's a long drive. I've got a lot to do before I leave for Paris."

"Aren't you going to say good-bye to Dad?"

She could hardly marshal her thoughts. Eyes level with his chest, she watched the rise and fall of the hard muscles under the mat of blond hair. All she could think of was the feel of those muscles pressing against her. She tore her eyes away and stared at the ground. "I left a note on the kitchen table."

There seemed to be nothing else to say. She opened the car door and slid in, fiddling with the lights and windshield wipers until she established some shaky control over her voice. "Good-bye, Joe."

"Is this what you'd do if we were married—take off for Europe after our first big fight?" She had never heard his voice so quiet, and she suspected that when Joe got really mad he didn't yell—he did just what he was doing now. "Well?" he demanded. "Are you going to run out on me?"

"Since you can't deal with my money, I'm taking it as far away from you as I can," she said, her voice quiet. "Maybe if I spend enough of it, I can get it down to a sum you won't find objectionable."

"Sara!"

But she was pulling away, determined not to let him see her cry. Through a watery haze she recognized Bailey's beat-up Hornet pulling into the drive, and she gave him a shaky nod as he passed, staring at her curiously. Joe Dancy's home for lost souls was losing one inhabitant and gaining another.

She drove as far as Keokuk, fighting exhaustion every mile of the way. At last she could go no farther. The hell with pushing herself to the limit! She pulled into a motel as daylight was breaking and roused the manager from sleep. Sara had never felt so tired in her life.

But she'd hardly fallen asleep before she was awake again. She glanced at her watch, annoyed. It was six, about the time Joe usually came into her bedroom on some pretext or other to wake her up, usually bringing coffee and something to eat. "Damn, damn, damn!" she muttered into her pillow, starting to cry again. *I like beautiful clothes*, she told herself. *I love fine Swiss chocolate. I don't belong with a man who eats egg sandwiches with ketchup. And thinks wealth is a social disease. But, Lord, it was wonderful while it lasted.* And with that thought she dropped into sleep again.

She fell instantly into a confused dream. Lost and frightened, she couldn't remember who she was. She wandered through a crowd of strangers, feeling totally alone and bereft. Suddenly Joe appeared, holding out his arms. "You're my Sara," he said softly, "and I love you." Everything was all right then. She woke up with the most incredible aching loneliness.

She realized in that single moment that she had been running out on more than Joe. She'd deserted herself, too. Maybe she felt she didn't deserve to be happy with Joe, after what happened with John. But it was her own happiness she was running out on . . .

She didn't need designer suits. She didn't need Paris. She didn't need Swiss chocolates—well, maybe once in a while. But she needed Joe! And if money was the problem, then she'd just have to get rid of it. She was going to make Joe see that the money didn't matter, if she had to club him over the head. He could be *so* obstinate! She was determined to point that out to him, too, as she threw back the sheet and began to dress in jeans and sneakers. She brushed her hair and let it fall loose. She planted her hands on her hips and addressed her reflection in the mirror. "So you don't want my money, Joe Dancy. Well, fine and dandy. I'll just bury it in a hole somewhere. But one thing you're going to get is me!"

This time she felt nothing like the Lone Ranger as she drove to the farm. She was Juliet running to Romeo,

Cinderella racing to Prince Charming... That she was planning to hit Prince Charming over the head, if necessary, was of no importance. He was still the man she loved more than anything or anyone else.

She knew she was coming home at last when she turned into the drive under the Twin Oaks sign.

Joe's truck was parked in front of the house. She got out and stretched, half hoping he would come galloping out of the house and make this easier for her. But he didn't. So she tentatively pushed open the screen door, calling softly, "Joe?" He wasn't in the house. The aroma of coffee still hung in the air, and a half-eaten cherry turnover sat on the kitchen table. She ran her finger over the icing and smiled.

She went out, closing the screen door behind her softly. She heard a tractor and followed the sound till she caught sight of the clumsy vehicle making neat rows in the field. Her heart had skipped a beat before she realized that Eddie was in the driver's seat. She turned a corner of the house and stopped a minute to stare out over the meadow with its Venus looking glass. A cow glanced up at her and bawled.

"Get out of here, Dunbar!" a voice rang out across the field. "I don't need trouble from you, too!" The angry shout was followed by squawking and a clatter of wings.

She knew where he was now. She circled around the grapevines, and caught sight of him as she passed the last cluster of vines. He stood with his back to her, brushing dirt from his hands. Dunbar had settled his offended feathers in a limb above and was loudly, piercingly, chewing Joe out. Sara let her eyes feast on the man she loved. He was wearing faded jeans, and her blood heated as her eyes roved over his hips and thighs. He'd been working—she saw the evidence in the sweat-streaked black T-shirt that had worried its way out of his waistband, and in the gasoline-powered tiller lying by the grapevines where he had apparently abandoned it.

She didn't know what to say, so she didn't say anything. She bent and picked up a handful of moist dirt, molding it into a ball in her hands. Then she pitched it at his back.

It splattered on his shoulder with a satisfying thwack, and immediately he spun around. When he saw Sara, something sparked in his eyes. But he clamped his mouth shut and jammed his hands in his pockets, half turning away from her. Sara planted her hands on her hips and eyed him warily.

"It means Watchful Fox," he said at last.

"What?"

"Keokuk. That's what it means. It was named after Chief Keokuk of the Fox tribe. He's buried there."

"Oh."

"Well, I thought you might want to know. It seemed to be on your mind last night."

"I had a lot on my mind last night."

He cleared his throat. "I thought you'd be in Europe by now."

"I would have been," she said softly. "But I forgot my purple parrots."

"Oh." He dug his toe into the soft ground, staring down at his shoes. "Sara, about the money..."

"I'll give it up," she said immediately. "Along with suits and high heels. And I'm not going to Europe."

"You mean that?" He beamed. "I was wondering when you'd come to your senses. But"—his voice sobered—"happy as I am about Paris, Sara, there's still a little problem with the money." He frowned, scratching the back of his neck. He hadn't shaved yet, and blond stubble glinted as his head came up.

"Now, listen," she began, not looking at him as she launched into her explanation, so carefully rehearsed during her drive. "I was being unreasonable. I won't say another word about the loan from Carol. You have a right to make whatever arrangements you want, where the farm is concerned. But I've decided to burn all my money. We'll make a bonfire and roast hot dogs over the flames."

He stared at her, not speaking for a moment. "Unless you want our children to grow up penniless," he said at last, a gleam in his eye, "you're going to have to give me the money after all. I didn't sign the paper for Carol's loan."

"For heaven's sake, why not?" she demanded. "You really are crazy. You know that?"

An abashed smile was playing at the corners of his mouth. "Well, yes, I guess I am. But I realized there was a lot of truth in what you said last night. It was pride that made me refuse your money. I worked hard for my own money, playing baseball. And I plowed every last cent of it into the farm. I guess I plowed a lot of myself into the farm, too. You were right—I couldn't accept the thought that you could come along with your fancy inheritance and bail me out."

"And now you've accepted it?" she ventured.

He was burying his toe in the dirt again and rubbing his knuckles against his jeans. "Yeah. I thought about it." He paused. "And Dad told me I was a damn fool. So did Miss Mary and Bailey. By the way, Bailey dropped in just after you left. Apparently he'd gone to see my friend after all. Hell—now he has a job."

Sara smiled. "I'm glad to hear it."

"I think Staff was mad at me, too. He stared me down like a dead fish."

"Probably smelled like one, too," she observed. Something else occurred to her. "What . . . what did you say about children?"

"Children?" He was really working to hide his grin now, rubbing his chin and pretending to search his memory.

"Joe Dancy, so help me I'm going to throw dirt at you again!" she threatened. Dunbar added his screech from the tree.

The threat worked. Joe started to laugh. "Yeah, our kids," he said. "I figured your money belonged to them as much as to me. The farm, too. So I guess there's nothing wrong with using the money on the farm."

"Children," she repeated. "You mean you want to marry me?"

"Well, sure, unless you want to have kids without getting married. I mean, a woman like you, who hates to be pushed into anything—"

He didn't get any farther because she launched herself at him and fell full force into his arms. He loosed his laughter again and swung her in a circle. "Imagine!" he crowed. "Our children!"

"Little champion Niblets!" she chimed in.

"Kernels," he corrected her lazily, his mouth descending to hers.

"Mmmm," she murmured against his lips. "Frank's Fertilizer."

"What?" He raised his head quizzically.

"You remind me of Frank's Fertilizer," she said mischievously. "The one with pow."

Chuckling, he drew her back to him, giving her a kiss that went beyond pow and straight into the realm of magic. The breeze picked up and moved over them like a whispered blessing, and from his perch Dunbar screeched. Sara was home.

# SECOND CHANCE AT LOVE

## COMING NEXT MONTH

**TANGLING WITH WEBB #346 by Laine Allen**
Writer's block drives whimsical Cristy McKnight
to a rash wager with wickedly handsome, infuriatingly
smug Webster Cannon: She'll concoct his
mystery if he'll pen her romance!

**FRENCHMAN'S KISS #347 by Kerry Price**
So what if he makes beautiful music, cooks
divinely, and kisses exquisitely? Thoroughly
unpredictable French composer Jean-Claude Delacroix
is *not* the reliable companion Sherry Seaton requires.

**KID AT HEART #348 by Aimée Duvall**
Where toy designer Lisa Fleming goes,
chaos follows—to the chagrin...and delight...
of toy company owner Chase Sanger, who begins
to hope he's found a lifelong playmate!

**MY WILD IRISH ROGUE #349 by Helen Carter**
Darkly handsome, joyfully spontaneous,
Liam Claire teases and tempts reserved Ingrid Peterson,
pursuing her across Ireland until she's nervous,
confused...and *very* aroused!

**HAPPILY EVER AFTER #350 by Carole Buck**
Lily Bancroft will do anything to get
the money—even dress as Snow White—but nothing
on earth will ever turn ruthlessly powerful
Dylan Chase into a fairy-tale prince.

**TENDER TREASON #351 by Karen Keast**
Wealthy, elusive, dictatorial Nyles Ryland electrifies
insurance investigator Lauren Kane with silken caresses
and drugging kisses. But she has no intention of playing
this week's lover to Grand Cayman's mystery man...

# SECOND CHANCE AT LOVE

## Be Sure to Read These New Releases!

SWANN'S SONG #334 by Carole Buck
Knowing both karate and kids, Megan Harper poses
as a nanny to secretly guard rock star Colin Swann and
his irrepressible son...and gets into deep
trouble when love complicates the deception!

STOLEN KISSES #335 by Liz Grady
Mattie Hamilton is rehearsing a museum
heist when tuxedo-clad thief Devlin Seamus Devlin
tackles her in midair...and offers to tutor
her in *all* kinds of midnight maneuvers!

GOLDEN GIRL #336 by Jacqueline Topaz
In sophisticated Hollywood, schoolteacher Olivia Gold
finds both her movie star grandmother *and* dashing soulmate
Andrew Carr—who transforms her into a glittering
golden girl and spellbinds her with sensual enchantment.

SMILES OF A SUMMER NIGHT #337 by Delaney Devers
Like a modern rogue, plantation owner
Jules Robichaux sweeps April Jasper away with cynical
charm, smoothly seduces her under moonlit
magnolias...but won't trust her enough to offer his love.

DESTINY'S DARLING #338 by Adrienne Edwards
"Bought" by ex-husband Bart Easton at a charity
benefit, Dot Biancardi recalls poignant moments—of
gallant courtship, wedded bliss...and lonely
heartache. Dare she risk repeating past mistakes?

WILD AND WONDERFUL #339 by Lee Williams
Trapped on a wild Maine island with brawny recluse
Greg Bowles, who's rejected the inheritance she's come to
give him, heir hunter Alicia Saunders finds a new
tension building...desire quickening.

**Order on opposite page**

# SECOND CHANCE AT LOVE

| | | |
|---|---|---|
| ___ 0-425-08750-6 | SWEETS TO THE SWEET #311 Jeanne Grant | $2.25 |
| ___ 0-425-08751-4 | EVER SINCE EVE #312 Kasey Adams | $2.25 |
| ___ 0-425-08752-2 | BLITHE SPIRIT #313 Mary Haskell | $2.25 |
| ___ 0-425-08753-0 | MAN AROUND THE HOUSE #314 Joan Darling | $2.25 |
| ___ 0-425-08754-9 | DRIVEN TO DISTRACTION #315 Jamisan Whitney | $2.25 |
| ___ 0-425-08850-2 | DARK LIGHTNING #316 Karen Keast | $2.25 |
| ___ 0-425-08851-0 | MR. OCTOBER #317 Carole Buck | $2.25 |
| ___ 0-425-08852-9 | ONE STEP TO PARADISE #318 Jasmine Craig | $2.25 |
| ___ 0-425-08853-7 | TEMPTING PATIENCE #319 Christina Dair | $2.25 |
| ___ 0-425-08854-5 | ALMOST LIKE BEING IN LOVE #320 Betsy Osborne | $2.25 |
| ___ 0-425-08855-3 | ON CLOUD NINE #321 Jean Kent | $2.25 |
| ___ 0-425-08908-8 | BELONGING TO TAYLOR #322 Kay Robbins | $2.25 |
| ___ 0-425-08909-6 | ANYWHERE AND ALWAYS #323 Lee Williams | $2.25 |
| ___ 0-425-08910-X | FORTUNE'S CHOICE #324 Elissa Curry | $2.25 |
| ___ 0-425-08911-8 | LADY ON THE LINE #325 Cait Logan | $2.25 |
| ___ 0-425-08948-7 | A KISS AWAY #326 Sherryl Woods | $2.25 |
| ___ 0-425-08949-5 | PLAY IT AGAIN, SAM #327 Petra Diamond | $2.25 |
| ___ 0-425-08966-5 | SNOWFLAME #328 Christa Merlin | $2.25 |
| ___ 0-425-08967-3 | BRINGING UP BABY #329 Diana Morgan | $2.25 |
| ___ 0-425-08968-1 | DILLON'S PROMISE #330 Cinda Richards | $2.25 |
| ___ 0-425-08969-X | BE MINE, VALENTINE #331 Hilary Cole | $2.25 |
| ___ 0-425-08970-3 | SOUTHERN COMFORT #332 Kit Windham | $2.25 |
| ___ 0-425-08971-1 | NO PLACE FOR A LADY #333 Cassie Miles | $2.25 |
| ___ 0-425-09117-1 | SWANN'S SONG #334 Carole Buck | $2.25 |
| ___ 0-425-09118-X | STOLEN KISSES #335 Liz Grady | $2.25 |
| ___ 0-425-09119-8 | GOLDEN GIRL #336 Jacqueline Topaz | $2.25 |
| ___ 0-425-09120-1 | SMILES OF A SUMMER NIGHT #337 Delaney Devers | $2.25 |
| ___ 0-425-09121-X | DESTINY'S DARLING #338 Adrienne Edwards | $2.25 |
| ___ 0-425-09122-8 | WILD AND WONDERFUL #339 Lee Williams | $2.25 |
| ___ 0-425-09157-0 | NO MORE MR. NICE GUY #340 Jeanne Grant | $2.25 |
| ___ 0-425-09158-9 | A PLACE IN THE SUN #341 Katherine Granger | $2.25 |
| ___ 0-425-09159-7 | A PRINCE AMONG MEN #342 Sherryl Woods | $2.25 |
| ___ 0-425-09160-0 | NAUGHTY AND NICE #343 Jan Mathews | $2.25 |
| ___ 0-425-09161-9 | ALL THE RIGHT MOVES #344 Linda Raye | $2.25 |
| ___ 0-425-09162-7 | BLUE SKIES, GOLDEN DREAMS #345 Kelly Adams | $2.25 |

---

*Available at your local bookstore or return this form to:*

**SECOND CHANCE AT LOVE**
*THE BERKLEY PUBLISHING GROUP, Dept. B*
*390 Murray Hill Parkway, East Rutherford, NJ 07073*

Please send me the titles checked above. I enclose _____. Include $1.00 for postage and handling if one book is ordered; 25¢ per book for two or more not to exceed $1.75. New York residents please add sales tax. Prices are subject to change without notice and may be higher in Canada.

NAME _____

ADDRESS _____

CITY _____ STATE/ZIP _____

(Allow six weeks for delivery.)                    SK-41b

# A STIRRING PAGEANTRY
# OF
# *HISTORICAL ROMANCE*

### Shana Carrol
___ 0-515-08249-X  Rebels in Love                $3.95

### Roberta Gellis
___ 0-515-07529-9  Fire Song                      $3.95
___ 0-515-08600-2  A Tapestry of Dreams           $3.95

### Jill Gregory
___ 0-515-07100-5  The Wayward Heart              $3.50
___ 0-515-08710-6  My True and Tender Love        $3.95
___ 0-515-08585-5  Moonlit Obsession              $6.95
       (A Jove Trade Paperback)
___ 0-515-08389-5  Promise Me The Dawn            $3.95

### Mary Pershall
___ 0-425-09171-6  A Shield of Roses              $3.95
___ 0-425-09079-5  A Triumph of Roses             $3.95

### Francine Rivers
___ 0-515-08181-7  Sycamore Hill                  $3.50
___ 0-515-06823-3  This Golden Valley             $3.50

### Pamela Belle
___ 0-425-08268-7  The Moon in the Water          $3.95
___ 0-425-07367-X  The Chains of Fate             $6.95
       (A Berkley Trade Paperback)

### Shannon Drake
___ 0-515-08637-1  Blue Heaven, Black Night       $7.50
       (A Jove Trade Paperback)

---

*Available at your local bookstore or return this form to:*

 **BERKLEY**
*THE BERKLEY PUBLISHING GROUP, Dept. B*
*390 Murray Hill Parkway, East Rutherford, NJ 07073*

Please send me the titles checked above. I enclose _____ . Include $1.00 for postage and handling if one book is ordered; 25¢ per book for two or more not to exceed $1.75. California, Illinois, New Jersey and Tennessee residents please add sales tax. Prices subject to change without notice and may be higher in Canada.

NAME_____

ADDRESS_____

CITY_____ STATE/ZIP_____

(Allow six weeks for delivery.)